Single Dad's
WAITRESS

Single Dad's
WAITRESS

AMELIA WILDE

Dedication

To my husband, who takes our daughters out on breakfast dates all by his lonesome so I can write these stories. You are the greatest dad.

Contents

CHAPTER ONE 1

CHAPTER TWO 7

CHAPTER THREE.. 13

CHAPTER FOUR 19

CHAPTER FIVE.. 24

CHAPTER SIX 30

CHAPTER SEVEN 36

CHAPTER EIGHT 42

CHAPTER NINE... 48

CHAPTER TEN 54

CHAPTER ELEVEN.. 59

CHAPTER TWELVE.. 65

CHAPTER THIRTEEN 72

CHAPTER FOURTEEN... 78

CHAPTER FIFTEEN 85

CHAPTER SIXTEEN 91

CHAPTER SEVENTEEN 97

CHAPTER EIGHTEEN... 104

CHAPTER NINETEEN... 111

CHAPTER TWENTY 117

CHAPTER TWENTY-ONE... 124

CHAPTER TWENTY-TWO.. 131

CHAPTER TWENTY-THREE 137

CHAPTER TWENTY-FOUR 143

CHAPTER TWENTY-FIVE 149

CHAPTER TWENTY-SIX.. 155

CHAPTER TWENTY-SEVEN.. 161

CHAPTER TWENTY-EIGHT.. 167

CHAPTER TWENTY-NINE 173

CHAPTER THIRTY... 178

CHAPTER THIRTY-ONE 184

CHAPTER THIRTY-TWO 189

CHAPTER THIRTY-THREE... 195

CHAPTER THIRTY-FOUR.. 201

CHAPTER THIRTY-FIVE.. 206

CHAPTER THIRTY-SIX 211

CHAPTER THIRTY-SEVEN 216

CHAPTER THIRTY-EIGHT 221

CHAPTER THIRTY-NINE... 227

CHAPTER FORTY.. 232

CHAPTER FORTY-ONE 237

CHAPTER FORTY-TWO 242

CHAPTER FORTY-THREE.. 247

CHAPTER FORTY-FOUR... 252

CHAPTER FORTY-FIVE... 258

CHAPTER FORTY-SIX 264

CHAPTER FORTY-SEVEN 269

EPILOGUE 274

Chapter One

VALENTINE

I GRIN INTO THE GLEAMING REFLECTION OF THE GLASS LID perched on the stainless steel stockpot. I've got to force it this morning, and boy, is that a look. It's lucky that I can't actually see myself very clearly, what with the quartered potatoes bubbling under the lid, almost ready for the breakfast service.

I look *terrible*.

"What's the point?" I mutter the words at my roiling reflection.

"Tell me you're not talking to the potatoes." Gerald's gruff voice cuts through the low-level hum of the kitchen, and I try my best not to look like I've been caught red-handed talking to a starch when I straighten up. He steps in from the kitchen's side door, paper-wrapped packages filling his arms, and crosses to me, opening the walk-in fridge with his foot and disappearing inside.

"Not really."

When Gerald reemerges a few moments later, he has a plastic tray in his hands that's filled with sliced bacon. "It looked like you were talking to the potatoes."

"I was just trying to see if I look as shitty as I feel."

He shoots me a look. For a wizened chef, Gerald does not appreciate salty language, but it's true. I feel like shit. I'd blame Conrad Ford, my recently new ex-boyfriend, but he's only partly to blame. I was the idiot who thought he loved me.

What a ridiculous assumption.

Gerald puts the tray on the counter next to the griddle and starts laying out strips of bacon. He does it the same way every single morning. He's been doing it that way since I first got a job here in high school. I shouldn't have been surprised when I came back two weeks ago to find everything just how I left it. The only difference is that Gerald is eight years older. Not that you can tell by looking.

He flicks his eyes across the kitchen to me and lays out another row of bacon. "Is Sharon in yet?"

I open my mouth to answer him at the same time the front door to the restaurant opens, the bell chiming merrily against the glass. Sharon sweeps into the kitchen with an early morning summer smell clinging to her clothes, her dark hair piled high on top of her head. "Good morning, loves," she sings, breezing by to toss her purse into the tiny back office where she writes out our paychecks every Friday. "Everything good to go?" Her smile is so ungodly bright that I can't help but smile back, but the expression fades a little from her face when she finally gets a good look at me. "Looks like it's *not* good to go." She crosses her arms, cocking one hip to the side. "Spill it."

"Don't," says Gerald.

"It's nothing," I insist, pulling my apron off the hook on the wall next to Sharon's office. "Allergies."

She narrows her eyes. "You don't have allergies."

"Seasonal allergies."

"Valentine Carr, don't bullshit me."

Gerald sighs heavily, not looking at either of us, and Sharon rolls her eyes. They're not married, but they bicker like a couple that's been together for years—mostly through eye rolls and sighs.

I take my sweet time tying the apron around my waist. I can feel how puffy my eyes are every time I blink. Clearly, the concealer I applied so damn carefully this morning isn't doing a thing.

It's not that I don't want to tell Sharon what happened. It's just that the whole thing is so...*stupid*, so mortifying, that I'm not sure I can make my mouth form the words.

"Was it that asshole Conrad?"

The look on her face makes me burst out laughing. When I showed up here two weeks ago, fresh off a failed start to my would-be career in marketing and recently kicked to the curb by my boyfriend, Sharon gave me my old waitressing job back, no questions asked. Those came later, during the slow hours, when we wrapped silverware into napkins and wiped down the plastic menus with cleaning solution meant to kill the germs. She never said a word against Conrad then, but she didn't have to. She didn't even have to meet him. All she had to do was purse her lips and say *hmm* in that same old Sharon way.

"No," I finally manage to say. "Well, yes. But that was my fault. I should have seen it coming."

She waves her hands in the air like she's dispelling a bad cloud. "He wasn't worth your time. And he's not worth your tears."

Maybe not, but that doesn't make me feel better now. And tomorrow morning, when I wake up with that same pit in my stomach, it still won't help.

"I'm not crying."

Sharon cocks her head to the side. "We can all see your face, Valentine."

"Maybe I *was* crying because…" I want to say *because I'm back here working at a café when I was supposed to be starting a magnificent career*, but that would be a dick move. I also don't mention the fact that it doesn't make me proud to be living in one of my parents' cottages on their wide lakefront property. The Short Stack, after all, is Sharon's career, and Gerald's, too. It's only me who became too good for the place when I left for college.

Fine. I'll admit it. It stings that I had to come running back here with my tail between my legs. College was not the experience I thought it would be. I imagined I'd come out the other side confident and sure of myself and in possession of at least an entry-level job at a marketing firm.

I also imagined that Conrad wouldn't react the way he did to what happened.

Instead, I'm here, sliding my order pad into the pocket of my apron and getting ready to serve breakfast to a crowd of indeterminate size. It's Friday, so you never know how many people will show.

At least Sharon pays a decent wage, so I don't have to rely on tips. If I did, I might never save up enough to make it back out of here.

To where? The question thuds around in my brain.

"Cat got your tongue?" Sharon says, laughing, and then sweeps out toward the front of the restaurant. It's a tiny place, three rooms and a kitchen in what used to be a private house. A moment later, I hear her on the phone, talking to the guy who delivers the dairy products once a week. "—on your way?" There's a pause. "The side door. As usual." I'm still thinking of what to say when the bell tinkles against the glass, and Sharon greets the first customer of the day.

It's time to get my shit together.

I put a few pens into the pocket of my apron. The wood floor creaks under Sharon's feet while she seats whoever it is—probably a couple of old men, ready to camp out at a table with coffee for the first few hours of the morning—smooth my hands over my hair, and wash them one more time in the sink.

"Valentine will be right with you," says Sharon, loud and clear. That's my cue.

I move out to the front room, but my apron is wrong, somehow, despite all the time I took to tie it. Doesn't matter. I can do two things at once. "Good morning," I chirp, my hands working behind my back. I look down to make sure it's sitting just right. "Welcome to the Short Stack. I'm—"

That's when I look up and meet his eyes.

That's when everything changes.

Chapter Two

RYDER

"**P**ANCAKES!"

My daughter's voice rings out across the street and bounces back to us off the front wall of what seems to be the only place remotely like a diner in this entire godforsaken town. It doesn't even look like a diner—it looks like a house that's pressed up against the back side of the building that faces the main drag. It probably was a house, at one time or another, but all that matters to me right now is that they're open.

And that they serve pancakes.

It's been a long night, and not the fun kind. My eyes feel gritty, and there's an ache stretching across both of my shoulders. I'd give anything to crawl back into bed.

But Minnie's hungry. She's hungry for pancakes, and I don't have it in me to go to the store, wrestle her into the cart, and buy Bisquick. I'd rather take her out on a breakfast date.

"Look both ways," I say, and she swivels her head in two directions, not long enough to actually see if there are cars coming but enough to mimic the way that I look slowly, a few seconds in each direction. "No cars. It's safe. We can go." I'm not even thinking about the words coming out of my mouth. I must have said them a thousand times in the last year. Maybe a million. It's anyone's guess whether it will sink in.

It's anyone's guess whether any of this will turn out at all, but that's not a question for this fucking early in the morning.

It looks like a nice enough place, calm and warm in the early morning quiet.

We're definitely not in New York City. Not anymore. This is the kind of suburb where they've made a fetish out of nostalgia, and it grates on my nerves. It's too damn quaint. I miss the rush of the city, the grime, the way there was always noise. But try affording an apartment there with one salary, even if it's a decent one. And daycare on top of it.

What a joke.

This place is a joke, too. We're staying here one summer—exactly *one* summer—before Minnie and I are headed back out. I'm only here because I couldn't think of anywhere else to go after Angie fucked me over.

I shift Minnie into one arm and pull open the door to the cafe. A bell—a real, honest-to-god bell, not one of those electronic doorbells—chimes against the glass. The name of the place is printed on a custom sticker against the glass. Short Stack.

God.

I try not to roll my eyes. It's perfect for this town. I'm the misfit. But it's not going to do me any good to come off as the asshole the moment I step in the door. Especially not with a toddler in tow.

The first room in the cafe is a tiny one, with just enough room for a counter with a cash register and a case with what looks like fresh breads and scones. Minnie's hand, still chubby with baby fat, shoots out, finger extended. "Cookies?"

"Pancakes," I say it in as firm a tone as you can say the word *pancakes* in and turn away from the case, even though her toothy smile twists at my heart. It's damn difficult not to give her everything she asks for. She gives it one more chance, reaching for a flyer on a small notice board that hangs inside the doorway.

A middle-aged woman wearing all black appears from a doorway into the back—kitchen, I'm assuming—and at the sight of Minnie her face lights up. "Well, hello there." She somehow manages not to make it sound simpering, and I relax a little. Minnie is cute as hell, with blonde curls at the back of her neck, her hair fine and light, and big blue eyes. People can't resist her, but I'm not in the mood for a lot of attention. "Just the two of you?"

My hackles go up at the suggestion, even though I know it's fucking innocent. The other thing people can't resist? Asking me where my wife is. Whether she's on her way. If it's "just the two of us," I'm probably babysitting.

"Yes." I try not to sound like a total dick. I mostly fail.

It doesn't faze this woman at all. She snaps two menus out of a holder on the counter and smile at Minnie again. "You've got your pick—you're the first ones here this morning. My name is Sharon, by the way."

I nod, and her words sink in a moment later, along with the quiet calm of the place.

Oh, thank Christ. The last thing I want right now—honestly, the last thing—is to be surrounded by a clutch of old women who want to do shit like pinch Minnie's cheeks and talk to her incessantly throughout the meal. My daughter is pretty good for a toddler. She knows how to eat in a restaurant. She knows how to charm the hell out of everyone she meets.

I'm the one with frustration boiling under the surface, and it's nobody's fault except Angie's.

Maybe mine.

But that's beside the point. The point right now is breakfast. The point right now is to divide up last night from the rest of the day, hitting a reset on everything so we can just get through it.

We follow Sharon into the second room. This place really is tiny—a small entryway with the counter, the front room, and a room in the back. The room in the back is painted a deep orange that somehow doesn't look completely fucking hideous, and the room in front is bathed in light from a picture window.

"Do you want to sit in the orange room or by the window?"

Minnie doesn't hesitate. She points to that big window, where we'll be on display for this entire town to see. "Window!"

"Okay."

Sharon reappears with a high chair, sweeping the second chair away from the window two-top before I can get to it. I don't need her help, but she's too damn efficient. I get Minnie into the seat and buckle her in while Sharon heads back toward the front counter. I'm just taking my seat when her voice cuts across the room, loud and clear. "Valentine will be right with you."

Valentine must be the waitress, and I can't help but be relieved. *Valentine* sounds like a quiet, middle-aged woman who won't drive me insane by the end of the meal or try to give me her number.

"Daddy—" Minnie is reaching for a basket with little plastic containers of jam.

I put my hand on hers and pretend to shake it. "We'll get pancakes in just a minute."

"Good morning." The voice doesn't sound middle-aged. "Welcome to the Short Stack." There's another woman coming through the door, eyes on her apron, and holy *shit* she's not middle-aged. She's young and gorgeous, and her auburn hair is pulled

11

into a shining bun on the top of her head, perfect somehow even though it's that messy style that I can't stand. That I usually can't stand, anyway. "I'm—"

She brings her hands around in front of her, reaching for her notepad, and her eyes come up to meet mine. They're green and clear and huge, and they go wide at the sight of me, her words stopping abruptly.

My heart pounds in my chest. I want to look away, but I can't. I absolutely can't.

Oh, shit.

Chapter Three

VALENTINE

THE GUY SITTING AT THE FRONT TABLE—MY FAVORITE TABLE in the house—isn't one of a crowd of old men who will require constant tending and refill after refill of coffee while I dodge hands that "accidentally" reach towards my ass. He's not an old man at all.

He's the sexiest man I've ever seen. Sexiest person, if I'm being honest, and one look into his blue eyes has heat rushing down my spine and up into my cheeks.

I was saying something. What was I saying? I have to keep saying it—that's what I'm here to do—but he's scowling at me, looking at me with a certain darkness in his blue eyes, and it's utterly captivating and terrifying all at once.

He's not alone.

That fact hits me a few long heartbeats later, when the tiny figure in the high chair facing the window spins around, a big grin on her face. "Heyo," she says, waving a chubby hand in the air at me. "Pancakes. Pancakes, pease."

Snap out of it, Valentine. A toddler I can handle, and at least she's forced my gaze to her so I can suck in a deep breath.

"Wow," I say, my voice way too high. I sound like an idiot. I clear my throat, but my entire body is pulsing with the sight of this man, the energy radiating off of him and filling the entire front room of the Short Stack. I have to get it together. "Pancakes coming right up." Oh, shit. Should I be taking an order from a toddler without even getting permission from—well, he must be her dad, if he's here with her, especially this early. He looks young to be a dad, but then again—

It takes everything I have to look back into his smoldering eyes. "Let me start over." I'm practically choking on every single word out of my mouth, and I have no idea why. "I'm Valentine, and I'll be taking care of you this morning."

"Great." His voice is low and gruff, a little gravelly, like he's short on sleep. If he has a toddler, he's probably always short on sleep. My mind spins into overdrive. I have no idea who this man is, and I've never heard of him before. He must be new in town, because I can't imagine that the old biddies who come in around ten on the weekdays would keep him a secret if he were one of

14

their grandsons. He reaches for a menu, his muscles flexing beneath the fabric of his gray T-shirt, and suddenly I can't breathe again.

"Pancakes?" His daughter is looking at me with the most charming grin I've ever seen on a child. I have to resist the urge to sit down next to her and strike up a conversation because I'm pretty certain it would be the cutest damn thing ever to grace the face of the earth.

"You did a good job ordering pancakes, Minnie," he says to her, eyes moving over the print on the menu. "I'll have the All-American breakfast." He gathers up the other menu, and that's when I realize I'm still standing in the middle of the room like an idiot.

I move closer to the table, which is like throwing myself into the surface of the sun. I take the menus, and one falls out of my hands and back onto the table. The little girl bursts out laughing, the sound pure delight. "You drop it." She points at the menu and I grin down at her while I pick it up.

"I did drop it, yes." God, my voice sounds so weird and strange that I can hardly believe it's mine. I turn my attention back to this man—this unbelievably hot man—and try again. "You said the All-American, right? White, wheat, or rye for the toast?"

"Rye." He doesn't return my smile, though the corner of his lip quirks upward a little.

"And did you want hash browns or American potatoes?"

"I thought it was the All-American breakfast."

My face can't get any hotter, but then it does. "Well, it is, but we offer two kinds of—"

"I know. I was joking."

"Oh." I laugh, but it sounds nervous. I wanted it to sound confident. "I couldn't tell there for a minute." And now I just sound hokey and small town and like everything I don't want to be in this moment. In this moment I want to be so irresistible that he can't help but get up from the table, take me by the hand, and...

...and what? Abandon his ridiculously cute daughter in the middle of the restaurant, not to mention any other customers that might come in and need my waitressing skills?

Not going to happen. Not now, not ever.

"Hash browns."

"Great choice!"

His eyes are so blue. They're like the ocean. They're like the lake on a calm day. They're like a million clichés, only they're alive in a way that I've never seen before. Alive and unhappy. Alive and almost tortured, his expression is so intense. I could just fall into those eyes.

Which is exactly what happens.

I'm in the middle of trying to decide whether his eyes are more sky-like or ocean-like when his daughter leans forward and sticks her face into my field of vision, her head almost parallel with the table. "Thank you!" She chirps the words, waving her hand, and I realize I've been standing here, silent, staring at this man for so long that I'm surprised he didn't say a thing.

And now I've been dismissed by a toddler.

"You're so welcome!" I tell her, wishing desperately that the blush would disappear from my cheeks, and turn on my heel.

I'm three steps toward the door when it hits me—I didn't ask him about his eggs, and Jesus, it's painful, having to stop and turn around with his eyes still burning into my back.

He's still not smiling, but he *is* looking at me, his arms crossed over his chest, something close to a smirk on his face.

I clear my throat. "Oh, and there was one more thing."

He raises his eyebrows. "I'm not giving you my number." His tone is so flat that I know it's not a joke. Not this time.

"I wasn't going to—" I swallow my pride and the sudden wound rising in my chest, because *damn,* was that an asshole thing to say. Only every nerve is so alive with him that I can't think of anything to say back. I'm lost for a witty retort. "How do you like your eggs?"

Something flashes through his expression—guilt?—but he doesn't apologize. He's going to say that he likes them fertilized, isn't he? I almost laugh out loud at the joke he hasn't made, that he wouldn't make, not with that brooding attitude. Eggs. Focus on the eggs. "Over easy."

"Great." It's a real effort to get the words out now. "I'll be right back with that pancake."

I'm in the kitchen before it comes to me. *I wouldn't take your number even if you gave it.*

Damn it.

Chapter Four

RYDER

THE SECOND SHE DISAPPEARS BACK INTO THE KITCHEN, HER shoulders tense beneath her black T-shirt, I sag against the seat and suck in a deep breath. It's like all the air is flooding back into the room.

I run a hand through my hair, and Minnie finally achieves her main goal since we've walked into the restaurant. She overturns the holder in the middle of the table and clutches a packet of grape jelly in her little fist. "Help me?" She holds out the packet, her eyes big and blue, a little grin on her face. My heart literally gets warmer, though it's hard to tell beneath the fire that's rushing through my entire body.

I don't want Valentine, the waitress at the Short Stack, this strange cafe in a town I don't want to live in. I don't want anything to do with her. I especially don't want her to come back out here and smile at me the way she was smiling at me before, somehow shy and confident at the same time. I *definitely* don't want to wrap one arm around her waist and steer her toward the back of this place, where I'm sure there's some sickeningly charming bathroom that I can take her into and lock the door behind us, push her up against the wall, and—

"Daddy, help!" Minnie waves the jelly insistently at me, pushing it toward me, and I take it in my hand, pulling at the plastic corner. This isn't the kind of thing I normally let her do in a restaurant, but my head is a blur, and I have to collect myself before Valentine comes back.

Why did I have to be such a dick?

Not that it matters. I'm going to give her a big tip, and then I'll be on my way. We're never going to see each other again after this.

I laugh out loud at the thought. It'll be work to avoid her in a town this size. Valentine can't just work at the cafe twenty-four hours a day. She at least has to go grocery shopping, and there's only one place in town that's not so expensive it makes my head spin.

I close my eyes for a few moments.

"Spoon?" I unwrap a spoon from the napkin in front of Minnie's high chair and hand it to her. She digs into the jelly, beaming at me like I've handed her the keys to a kingdom a hell of a lot better than this place. "So good," she says, and I laugh again. The knot at the center of my gut untwists a little, like it always does when she smiles, when she laughs.

I don't know what I'm thinking, letting myself get swept away like this by the *waitress*, of all people. She's the last thing I need right now.

Now or ever.

Minnie points out the window. "I heard a doggie! Barking!"

"Do you see a dog?"

Focus. Focus on the only person who matters in the entire world.

I carry on a conversation with Minnie about the dog, which comes into view a minute later. It's a golden retriever, clearly excited as hell to be alive. I can't say I felt the same when I walked into this cafe. The only thing I was excited about was the prospect of not having to make breakfast after the long hell that was last night. Listen, even if your daughter is cute as hell, when she decides she's afraid of her own blankets at two in the morning, after you've finally convinced yourself to fall asleep...

Well, she's only two. And here in the cafe, while she giggles and eats jam out of the container with a too-big spoon, I can't even be pissed at her.

"One pancake, coming up." Valentine sings the words like I didn't just dismiss her out of hand. My chest goes tight thinking about saying those words to her, but I can't force an apology out of my mouth. Her face is still scarlet, but she puts the plate delicately on the table just out of Minnie's reach.

When Minnie sees the pancake, it's like she's won the lottery. She clutches her small fists in front of her and grins so wide I can see almost all of her teeth. "Mickey Mouse!" She points at the pancake, which is, no shit, in the shape of a Mickey Mouse, with a whipped cream smile on it. "A happy face!"

"It *is* a happy face!" Valentine exclaims, her eyes going wide like she's just noticing the whipped cream for the first time. "You're a lucky girl!" She doesn't look self-conscious until she looks back at me, her mouth pressing into a thin smile like she's trying to play it cool and failing. "Your breakfast will be out in just a minute. I thought I'd bring the pancake out first, since—" She tries again. "I hope you don't mind waiting another minute."

"We don't have any other plans." I mean it to be lighthearted, some kind of a joke, but I'm so fucking terse instead that Valentine blinks. She doesn't flinch, but I see the falter in her smile, the flicker in her big green eyes.

I want to make her smile.

I want to do more than make her smile, but none of the things flying through my imagination are in any way appropriate for the Short Stack cafe.

"Well, that—that sounds like a relaxing day." Relaxing? With a two-year-old? I don't think so. "Do you like the beach?"

"Beach!" Minnie chirps, already digging her spoon into one of the whipped-cream eyes and putting it in her mouth as fast as she can. "Playground!"

"We do have a beach with a playground, right by the lake," says Valentine, looking at Minnie, who puts on her most beguiling expression.

"More ice cream?" Minnie holds up her hands in a plea sweet enough to break anyone's heart.

"Do you mean whipped cream?" says Valentine, cocking her head to the side.

"Yeah!"

Valentine looks back at me. "Is that okay?"

I put a smile on my face. I'm sure it looks hideous as hell. "Of course."

Valentine grins, and the sight of her smile makes my entire chest go warm. She disappears into the back, coming back a few moments later with an industrial-sized can of whipped cream in her hand. She holds it over Minnie's pancake. "Tell me when!" Minnie just claps her hands, giggling, and Valentine starts to put more whipped cream onto the pancake, the hiss of the can making Minnie laugh harder.

Then she says it—the thing I've been waiting for her to say all this time, the thing I've been dreading since I walked into this place, the thing that pisses me off, rage flooding my veins.

Chapter Five

VALENTINE

I KNOW IT'S A MISTAKE AS SOON AS THE WORDS ARE OUT OF MY mouth. His little daughter, Minnie—how fucking cute is that?—is laughing as I put dollop after dollop of whipped cream onto her pancake, and I'm so lost in the moment that I let them slip out without thinking, like some kind of idiot.

"Oh, your mom is going to be mad at me when you get home!"

I feel him tense. I don't have to look at him to know that he's gone stiff, his jaw clenched. The little girl doesn't seem to have heard me—she can't be more than two—but the shift in the air is like a cold front slamming into the restaurant and freezing my blood in my veins. Goose bumps prick at the back of my neck.

Do something. Do something, Valentine, before this turns into the most awkward moment in the history of the world.

"Listen," I say, straightening up, forcing myself to look into those endless blue eyes. The hard set of his chiseled jaw sends a shiver down my spine. He's *pissed*. "I shouldn't have assumed—"

I'm in such a hurry to get the words out that I completely forget about the whipped cream. I'm still holding it when my hands clench tightly because I'm so damn nervous, pressing down on the nozzle of the canister and spraying a hefty dollop right into the handsome stranger's face.

The entire world freezes.

His blue eyes go wide, the whipped cream stuck on the stubble on his cheek.

Holy shit.

What did I just do?

I'm torn between wanting to join in his daughter's laughter and wanting to run the hell away, as fast as my legs can carry me. Is he going to be livid? There aren't any other customers yet, but they could arrive any second to find this man shouting at me, or at least shouting at me for as long as Sharon would let him, which probably isn't very long.

"Daddy! Face!" Minnie's voice breaks into the moment, filled with glee. "Daddy's face!" she says again, and both of us look at her. The blonde curlicue at the back of her head shakes with laughter, and she waves her fork in the air, pointing it at her dad. Then the fork clatters to the floor, and she covers her mouth with her little hands, letting out a big belly laugh. "Daddy ice cream! Face!"

I look back at him just in time to see the shield over his face crack and crumble in the face of his daughter's laughter, and something in my heart surges with a warmth I have no business feeling about him or any other man at this point, really. He looks at the little girl and raises one eyebrow. "Is there something on my face?"

This is the new funniest thing she's ever heard, because she points again, giggling with her nose wrinkled. "Daddy's face!"

"What is it?"

He eggs her on, and suddenly I feel like an extra in a movie starring the two of them. What's my line? Do I just make a graceful exit back to the kitchen and go on with my life, like a normal person?

"I'm so sorry about that," I say as Minnie's laughter dies down and she reaches toward her plate, scooping up whipped cream with her finger and popping it into her mouth.

At the sound of my voice, I see his guard go back up—only not all the way. His shoulders aren't quite so tense. He narrows his blue eyes, and one corner of his mouth quirks upward in a smolder that's not quite a smile. A liquid heat spills down my spine.

"You too!" cries Minnie when she finally catches her breath. Her eyes are shining with laughter, and she stabs her finger in the air toward me, small eyebrows raised. "You too!"

"It's only fair." His voice is a smooth rumble, and when I look back at him I swear I feel it all the way down to my— "You put whipped cream on my face. She's right. You should have some on yours, too."

I raise my eyebrows back at Minnie and try to ignore the thunder of my heart. "I need some on my face, too?"

"Yes!" She throws her head back and claps her hands together. "Your face too!"

"Well, I guess—" I raise the canister toward my own cheek, slowly, slowly, and Minnie can't handle it. Peals of laughter ring out over the restaurant and for once I don't care if anyone else walks in.

"No way." He's a movement beside me, a strong, muscled movement in that t-shirt that clings to his biceps. I shouldn't swoon into his arms, right? That would be too much. That would just be too much. This man, with his blue eyes, with his unbelievable smirk, reaches for the oversized canister of whipped cream in my hands and plucks it away, then locks eyes with me.

I'm burning up. I'm going to burst into flames, my heart is beating so hard. But with a precision I've only seen in military men—he must be ex-military—he presses the nozzle of the canister and sprays a dollop onto two of his fingers. Then he reaches up, without a moment of hesitation, and presses them into my cheek.

Minnie goes wild. "Face! Face!"

It's at this moment, naturally, that Sharon steps back into the room, her face halfway between curiosity and irritation. She likes the sound of happy customers, and Minnie is definitely one of those, but I'd bet anything that—

"Val, you've got orders waiting." Her eyes flick between me and the handsome stranger, who's still holding the whipped cream canister, and my face goes hot. I only have one order waiting, and it's his.

I choose not to comment on the whipped cream. "I'm on it," I tell her with a smile, which I keep on my face until she's back in the front room, out of sight. Then I wheel around. With whipped cream on his face and dancing eyes, he doesn't look nearly as intimidating as he did before. "You're going to get me in trouble."

"Me?" He points at his own chest, raising his eyebrows. "You're the one who sprayed a customer with whipped cream."

I think of his fingertips pressing against my cheek. I can still feel them there. I straighten my back and try to look imposing. "Are you going to complain?"

He considers me for a long moment. "Not this time."

Gerald's voice booms from the back. "Order up!"

"That's yours."

"You'd better go."

I turn away from him, but it's the last thing on earth I want to do.

Chapter Six

RYDER

MINNIE SPLASHES IN THE PUDDLE I DUG OUT FOR HER IN the sand on the lakeshore. She's into rocks lately—picking them up, stacking them, knocking down her towers—and this beach is perfect for that, by which I mean that it's rocky as fuck. The lake Valentine was talking about isn't like Lake Michigan, which was powerful and endless, roaring within a mile of the house I grew up in. No, this lake is more like a pond. But it's large enough that the water is clean, and there are rocks enough to keep Minnie entertained while I figure out what the hell we're going to do next.

The motel isn't working out. Minnie needs more room. She

needs *a* room, so that we can both get some sleep at night. But I haven't been at the top of my game, so I don't have anything lined up. I didn't have anything lined up when I packed the car and drove out of the city a week ago, either. I only came here because I'm not going back to Michigan and my only family is here.

Not that I'm *that* interested in crawling back to my brother after all this time. All of this is only temporary, anyway. I just have to figure things out for the summer. One summer, and then we're headed out.

There's a Valentine in every town. The thought rings so stupidly false that I laugh out loud.

Minnie splashes her feet into the shallow puddle, and then points down to it. "It's wet."

"It's a puddle."

"Puddle."

She's quite the conversationalist.

Step one: find a place to live. Step two: find a job. Step three: stop thinking about Valentine.

The only problem is that in order to tackle steps one and two, I have to bump step three up the list. Only I can't get her out of my head. Granted, it's only been a couple of hours, but I can't stop going over her curves in my mind, the silky sound of her voice, the way her red hair glinted in the sun coming through the cafe window, copper strands shot through it. I want to go back there right now and untwist her hair from its holder and run my fingers through it. I want it so badly that I almost tell Minnie to leave the rocks.

The rest of breakfast was smooth as hell, which was almost a disappointment. By the time Valentine came back with my plate there were other people filing in, and she couldn't spend any more time screwing around with me. I finally had to wipe the whipped cream off my face. Minnie kept trying to flag Valentine down for more, and in the end, I had to whisk her out to avoid a total melt-down. Valentine had dropped the bill on the table on the way to drop off an entire tray's worth of food to a group in the back, and damn if I didn't want to wait for her to come back.

But nobody wants a toddler screaming in their ear, so I paid at the front counter and headed out.

I run my hands through my hair. For once in the last three months, my jaw doesn't feel tight and aching. This town isn't my favorite, but suddenly there's possibility.

And it's *not* because I've fallen for a waitress. It's definitely not. I don't know that many people who've been able to recover from embarrassment like she did back there, and at least she's given me a glimmer of home that this summer won't be a total fucking disaster.

Minnie raises her head from the sand, squints, and then takes off running on her two-year-old legs. She looks almost like a kid now, not just the chubby baby she seemed like when she was up in the middle of last night.

"Minnie—"

She's not going far, skidding to a stop after only a few steps. She squats down, peering at something on the ground.

"What are you looking at?" My heart is beating a little faster, just from watching her run. I'm ready to take off after her. I'm ready to do whatever it takes to protect her, and even though she's only gone a few feet, my muscles are tensed. Still, I don't want her to think I'm some raging psycho, so I keep my tone even and relaxed.

"Paper." Paper. She picks up a torn shred of paper from the sand and unrolls it, then comes back across to me. "Here you go." She holds it out to me.

"Thanks, honey." It's trash—a section of rolled-up newspaper—but it reminds me of something. It reminds me of Minnie's hands reaching for that message board in the cafe, the one with all those flyers fastened to it with push pins.

I leap up from the sand. Shit. Is anyone around to have witnessed that? I don't actually have fire ants down my boxers.

"Minnie, let's go."

She grins up at me, holding her arms up to be lifted. I scoop her up and start making a beeline for the car, which is in an empty row of the parking lot. We've got to go across a wide green expanse of grass, nothing like the deserts in Afghanistan, before we get there.

It takes forever to buckle Minnie into her car seat, even though she's not even putting up a fuss. It's just that my hands don't want to work. I want to be driving already, heading back for that cafe—heading back for the waitress named Valentine. I want to touch the smooth skin of her cheek without whipped cream on my hands.

But no—I'm not going back there for her. I'm going back there for that message board. If there's anywhere in town that will have information on a place for us to live, it'll be that message board. I'm sure of it.

Finally I get everything clipped and buckled and throw myself into the front seat.

"Daddy!" Minnie cries.

My mind races through all the things I could have forgotten to do, and I whip around. "What is it, doll?" She grins at me for a long, silent moment, and I take a deep breath. Patience. Fucking patience. "What do you need, Minnie?"

She extends her hand, leaning forward against the straps of her car seat. "Here. Here you go, Daddy."

I reach back and open my hand, and she drops something into my palm—a treasure from the beach. It's a piece of beach glass that's perfectly worn by the water, all the edges smooth, a gleaming green like Valentine's eyes. "Is this for me?"

Minnie grins wider. "For you, Daddy."

My heart melts. Last night doesn't matter. All that matters is finding this sweetheart a nicer place than the motel by the highway to live in.

And if I happen to see Valentine while I do it, I guess that would be fine.

I start the car and put it into gear. "Do you want to go back to the cafe, Minnie?"

"Yes!" she shouts, clapping her hands. "Right now! Right now!"

"Right now!" I shout with her, and then we're off.

Chapter Seven

VALENTINE

THE DOOR OF THE SHORT STACK SWINGS SHUT BEHIND THE last of the breakfast crowd, and I lean against the front counter.

That was a hell of a Tuesday morning. It felt like a Saturday rush, but I should have expected that. It's summer in Lakewood, and summer means tourists, and tourists mean weekdays that are just as hectic as the weekends.

I wonder if the sex god I saw earlier is a tourist. Well, *maybe* he's a sex god. There's really only one way to find out. My cheek still burns where he touched me—burns in a kind of pleasant hum. I wouldn't mind if he came back in and tried it again. Maybe if he came back in, I wouldn't act like such an idiot. God, what was I thinking? I lean my forehead into my fingertips.

"Did you get his number?" Sharon's voice makes me jump. I straighten up, spinning to face her.

"Do you have to sneak up on people like that?"

She waves a hand dismissively. "I never sneak anywhere, and you know it. What are you doing up here? Fantasizing about him?"

I cross my arms over my chest. "Fantasizing about who?"

Sharon clicks her tongue and reaches up to adjust her hair. The movement reminds me of my own hair, which has to look like a total mess after the breakfast shift. I take my own down, twisting it into a braid. There. Not quite so much pressure on my skull.

"You can't ignore my original question."

"I can and I will."

Sharon narrows her eyes. "Are you telling me that you didn't notice how attractive that guy was?"

"Are you telling me that you didn't notice how he has a *daughter*?"

She shrugs. "So what?"

"So—" How about, I'm just out of a relationship, and for related reasons? "He has a daughter. He's not interested in dating some waitress."

"Who said anything about dating?" Sharon smiles at me, her eyes twinkling. "I think you need to get out of this rut."

"I'm *not* in a rut. Conrad and I just broke up."

There's a small sink in the front corner, just near the counter with the cash register, and I move around to wash my hands.

"That may be," says Sharon sagely, "but Conrad was always an asshole. Forget about him. Move on. It's been forever."

"It's been six weeks."

"Six weeks, and you're still crying over him?"

I roll my eyes. "I'm not crying *now*. I was only crying this morning because—"

"That piece of shit called you up, didn't he?"

I can't answer her.

"You called *him*?" Sharon purses her lips. "Valentine. No. Focus on the here and now. Find out who that young man is."

"I'm not interested."

"You're a terrible liar."

Sharon takes her turn at the sink, washing up, and then leans on the counter over her elbows. I say nothing. I'm thinking of the sexy stranger, the way his muscles rippled under his T-shirt, the way those eyes were almost intoxicatingly blue. I'm thinking of his touch on my skin. No, I'm not interested. I can't get swept away by all that. Not now. I need time. I need to recover. I can't just go after a man I meet at work because—

Sharon laughs out loud. "Are you giving me the silent treatment?"

I laugh, too. "Not even. I was just mentally preparing to bus the last of the tables, and then—" I step over to the doorway into the next room, scanning the tables, pretending that's all that's on my mind.

"You were *not*. You were thinking about him. And who wouldn't be? You can admit it to me, Valentine." She's teasing, but my cheeks are getting red. "You can admit that he's the finest thing ever to walk in the front door. You can admit—"

I put both my hands on my hips, and Sharon laughs. "Fine, Sharon. Fine. I will admit it. I will admit that he was hot. And yes, I enjoyed looking at him. And yes, he might have been flirting with me just a little, but that doesn't matter because—"

The bell on the door chimes against the glass, and I turn on instinct, ready to greet whoever it is that's coming in for an early lunch.

Only it's not chiming because the door is just swinging open. It's chiming because a cute toddler named Minnie has flicked it up against the glass, reaching from her dad's arms. The door is wide open, and he's standing in the threshold, a half-smile on his face, looking right at me.

I open my mouth to welcome him back to the Short Stack, to make some witty comment about how he's only been gone a couple of hours and he can't possibly be hungry, but instead what comes out is: "Welcome, hungry already?"

His smile widens, and Sharon laughs out loud, taking over. "Welcome back. Did you forget something, or are you here for lunch?"

He doesn't take his eyes off me. "I'm here for your message board, actually."

"Come in, come in," says Sharon, making a sweeping gesture toward the shabby bulletin board. He steps inside, and his daughter grins at both of us. "Are you looking for anything specific?"

"A place to rent." He drops my gaze, turning to look at the flyers, and my stomach plummets into my shoes.

Because there *is* a flyer there with a place to rent. There's exactly one flyer, and I know exactly whose place it is.

"A place to rent!" Sharon exclaims. "Well, Valentine can tell you all about that."

He turns back, and I'm caught in his gaze. "Can she?"

I clear my throat. "It's very rude to talk about people like they're not in the room."

His blue eyes are, hot, hotter, the hottest. "I'm sorry about that. And—" He clears his throat. "I'm also sorry about being a d—" He stops himself just in time. Minnie has her arms wrapped around his neck, and she's staring right at me, but I'd bet a fat bundle that if he said the word "dick" right now, it would be a toddler disaster. "I'm sorry about how I acted earlier."

I shrug at him as awkwardly as is humanly possible. "Not a big deal. I shouldn't have said—"

"Don't worry about that. It's a mistake that everyone makes."

I don't want to think about what I said, and before I know it, the words are spilling out of my mouth. "I was *going* to say that I shouldn't have asked you how you like your eggs. You're clearly an over easy man."

"Oh? Is it that obvious?"

Jesus, that smoldering grin. It wipes my mind clean of everything I was about to say. "Y-yes." Lame. Can it get any more lame?

He laughs out loud, and Minnie does too, clapping her hand over her mouth. Sharon is leaning on the counter, hand under her chin, watching the entire thing like it's a shitty soap opera. I'm a terrible actress, and the longer he stands here, the hotter it's getting. "So," he says, and the way he says it makes me think he might ask me out on a date. I don't know how that would work, what with his daughter, what with *everything*, but suddenly I'm dying for him to ask me on a date so I can prove I'm not a tongue-tied nerd with a temporary waitressing job and not much else. "Tell me about this place for rent."

Chapter Eight

RYDER

"WE'RE SO GLAD TO HAVE YOU," THE OLD WOMAN SAYS tremulously, pressing the keys into my palm and squeezing with both hands like she's giving me a precious diamond. "If there's anything you need, anything at all, you don't hesitate to call me." She glances down at Minnie, holding my hand and standing still, a little shy in the presence of a seemingly ancient human, and gives her a watery smile. "And you, precious, you're going to love that little bedroom with the yellow walls. I just know it."

"Thanks, Mary." She finally drops my hand. "We'll be in touch."

She nods and ushers us back out the front door of her house, giving us a big wave while we head back out to the car.

"Thank you for your service, son," she calls out at the last minute. Old ladies can always tell. I wonder if it was obvious to Valentine that I was in the Army. It wouldn't be terrible if I stopped by the Short Stack one more time, would it?

Focus.

Step one, complete.

* * *

It was almost *too* easy, with Valentine's help. She'd stepped over to the notice board. In order to reach it, she'd had to stand right next to me, and damn it, I didn't want to move away. So I didn't.

Minnie was enthralled with her red hair, anyway, and the moment Valentine turned her eyes toward the message board Minnie's hands had shot out. "So pretty," she said, her small voice in my ear, and I'd had to agree with her. I could see Valentine's cheeks heating up, smell the scent of her hair, and God, there I was, getting more infatuated with the pretty waitress by the second.

Valentine reached out and gestured to a flyer pinned to the lower corner of the message board. This was no printed flyer—it was actually handwritten, in the spidery, precise handwriting of someone super old. *Cottage for rent to responsible individual. Two* *bedrooms. Across the street from the lake. $600/month.* The phone number at the bottom was guaranteed to be a land line. "This is probably the only place in town that's still available this far into the summer."

"Far? It's only June."

Valentine turned, crossing her arms over her chest, and narrowed her eyes. "It's the *third week* of June."

I looked back at her. "And?"

"Are you...new to town?" she asks the question like she already knows the answer.

I laughed. "I think we both know the answer to that."

It was her turn to chuckle. "True. I would have noticed if someone like you—" Valentine's face went absolutely scarlet. She cleared her throat, patting at her neck like something was caught there. "Most of the places were rented out months ago, but most people don't prefer to deal with land lines. Especially land lines without answering machines. The Culvers finally resorted to putting up this flyer." She'd taken a deep breath, her vivid green eyes sending sparks down my spine. "It's a cute little place, near the lake. Clean. They keep it well-maintained. I'm sure you'd like it..."

The pause was an invitation, and it struck me like a thick bolt of lightning that I hadn't offered her my damn name. "Ryder." I shifted Minnie's weight on my hip and stuck my hand out to Valentine. "Ryder Harrison."

She took my hand with a surprisingly strong grip, blushing even more furiously. "Valentine."

I didn't want to drop her hand, but I did. "I knew that already."

The little smile playing over her lips just about drove me crazy right there in the entryway of the Short Stack. "Valentine Carr."

"Valentine Carr." Sharon, the woman in black behind the counter, straightened up and moved into the kitchen, out of sight. "Tell me, Valentine Carr. Why do you know so much about this rental cottage?"

She looked me square in the eye and bit her lip, letting the question hang in the air for just a heartbeat. When she finally took in a breath it was like I felt it in my own lungs. "Well," she said, her voice smooth in my ears, "because it's right across the street from where I'm living."

* * *

The cottage is only a couple miles out of town, but it's all green out here—green leaves on the trees, green grass. I pull into the driveway, double-check the address, and get my first look at my new home.

Valentine was right. This might be a simple place—wood siding painted white, small and compact, with red shutters—but something about it makes me think it's the perfect summer place for me and Minnie.

And *not* because Valentine lives somewhere nearby.

I step out of the car and twist around, my hand on the back of my neck. The Culvers' property has a long front yard, ending in a two-lane road. There are two maple trees on the other side of the road, but beyond that, I can't see any houses.

I move one step toward the road. *Right across the street* clearly doesn't mean *right* across the street, so where the hell is Valentine's house?

Minnie sees me moving and screeches. "Daddy! No! Don't do that!"

Don't do that has to be one of my daughter's top ten phrases. I'm sure I'll appreciate it more when she's older. I open the back door and start unbuckling her belt. "Don't do what, Minnie?"

"Don't do that walking."

"I wasn't going anywhere."

When I lift her out of the car seat, she wraps her arms around my neck and leans her head into my shoulder. She must be damn exhausted because normally she'd be begging to walk by herself.

I take one last look across the street...but I can't. Not right now. I've got to get shit set up for Minnie.

I hold her in one arm while I pop the trunk, slinging two duffel bags and a Pack N' Play over my shoulder. We haven't been living with much.

"Baby doll," she says suddenly. The baby doll went everywhere with her right up until we came to Lakewood, and she just spied it in the trunk. I lean down, slowly, because I'm carrying all of our worldly possessions, and dangle her just close enough to grab it. She buries her face into my shoulder, and we head inside.

In less than ten minutes I have her bed set up, and she's napping, sound asleep. I go to check out the house.

Two bedrooms, one with a queen and one with a twin and a desk. A decent kitchen. A nice living room with a fireplace. A bathroom that looks like it was renovated fairly recently, and that's it. That's the whole place.

I can feel my shoulders relaxing. This kind of place? This is simple. This is easy.

Nothing like New York.

The furniture in the living room looks a little worn, but sturdy, and it's been carefully cleaned. I take a seat in a recliner by the window and settle in, letting out a sigh, breathing in the silence.

I watch the cars go by.

I tell myself again and again that I'm not looking for Valentine.

Chapter Nine

VALENTINE

IT's BEEN TWO DAYS, AND I HAVE NEVER BEEN MORE INVESTED IN my job at the Short Stack. This morning, I woke up an hour before my alarm and couldn't go back to sleep. I felt like a kid at Christmas, only I don't know if Christmas is actually coming.

Christmas being another appearance by Ryder Harrison, who has infiltrated all of my dreams.

Yesterday afternoon, when my shift was over, I'd made a point of driving down the road to my house at exactly the same speed I always drive. I am not going to be the kind of creeper who slows down to peer in the front windows of a rental cottage that he *might* be living in.

I'd be lying if I said my heart didn't speed up at the sight of the beat-up Chrysler in the driveway and the light spilling out into the yard.

My phone, ringing in my purse, ended up shattering the fantasy of baking something and taking it over, just on the off chance that it's really him. I'd pulled it out only to have my heart sink at the sight of Conrad's name on the Caller ID. Like a fool, I'd answered.

"Hello?"

"I'm going to need you to come get your things," he'd said, his voice clipped and flat.

"Things?" We'd had a long-distance relationship, Conrad and I, and I couldn't think of a single thing I'd left at his place in the city.

"There are some papers here. Records." He'd held his hand over the phone then, speaking to someone else in the background. My heart twisted in my chest. I'm supposed to be over him, but the sound of his voice, so dismissive, so damn rude, cut me to the core. "And a sweater."

Then I was pissed. "Conrad," I'd said, ice in my tone, "you could just mail those things to me." I don't give a damn about the sweater, not really, but the records.... I need those.

"You didn't leave a forwarding address, Valentine." He'd thrown the words at me like I'd been the one to break up with him, like I kicked *him* out.

"Do you have a paper and pen?"

"What? No, I—" He sighed heavily, like I was asking him to do something impossibly difficult. "Yes. Go ahead."

I rattled off my address, feeling like I was on a call with a snarky customer service representative. "I'll reimburse the shipping costs if you need me to."

He doesn't need me to, and we both know it. "That's fine," he said. "I'll put them in the mail."

"Thanks."

Then he'd ended the call with an abrupt *click*, leaving me feeling deflated, like a week-old party balloon. After that, I wasn't in the mood for baking. I especially wasn't in the mood to take a risk on a man. Even a man who looks like Ryder Harrison.

But this morning, my heart was beating hard before I even climbed out of bed. Once I did, there was no going back. A strange, giddy energy carried me all the way to the Short Stack. I was there before Gerald, even, and had to unlock by myself.

A full forty minutes of scrubbing down already-clean tables later, Gerald and Sharon showed up together, having the kind of loud conversation you only ever have if you think you're walking into an empty building. When Sharon saw me, she gasped. "Valentine, you scared the shit out of me."

I'd been working in the dark so as not to attract any early customers, and I had to laugh at Sharon's shocked face. "Sorry. Couldn't sleep."

She'd narrowed her eyes. "Why not?"

I shrugged, and I knew the instant I did it that it came off as totally unconvincing. "Just...ready to get a head start on the day."

She gave me a knowing smile and disappeared into the kitchen, shoulder to shoulder with Gerald.

I'm not fooling anyone. I can't even convince myself that I don't have a wild crush on a customer I've only seen once.

But he didn't show, not at breakfast, and not at lunch, and every time the door opened and it wasn't him, my heart sank a little more. Sharon saw.

"It's not personal, sweetheart," she told me when I was grabbing the last of the lunch orders. "Maybe he's just not hungry."

I rolled my eyes at her. "I am *not* waiting for him to show up."

I completely was.

* * *

I hang up my apron on the hook in the kitchen, wave goodbye to Gerald and Sharon, and head out onto the sidewalk. I parked at the local library today to get in a bit of a walk after work, but I haven't gone half a block before someone screeches my name.

"Val! *Val!*" I turn, a smile on my face before I even see hers. Cecily Harwood has been my best friend since the second grade, and here she is, screaming at me like I might not hear her in the midst of all this peaceful quiet. She comes barreling down the block at me, wrapping me in her arms like we haven't seen each other in weeks, squeezing tight.

"*Oof.* Let go of me, woman."

She holds me at arm's length like she's playing my mother on TV and looks me up and down. "Valentine, are you all right?"

If it were anybody else, I'd laugh in their face, but Cecily—Cece to just about everybody—is utterly sincere. She's sincere in a way that I can never seem to pull off. With me, it's all or nothing. Witty and cool, or totally awkward. "Yeah, I'm fine."

She clicks her tongue. "Seriously. Are you okay? I know you've only been back a couple weeks, but—"

Oh. So she's *not* talking about the fact that Ryder Harrison didn't show up at the Short Stack today. She's talking about Conrad. And moving back. And all of it. I haven't seen her since I got back to town, but I've kept her up to speed via text. About most things.

"Conrad called yesterday," I say, trying to keep things nonchalant but totally unable to keep a damn secret.

"He *did*?" Cece purses her lips. She disapproves of Conrad, no surprise, but alongside her sincerity, she loves gossip.

"Walk me to my car and I'll tell you about it."

She walks the next four blocks with me, and I tell her all about the asshole Conrad wanting me to drive several hours to pick up some papers and a *sweater,* for God's sake. "You should block him," she tells me when I'm done. "Block his number."

"I think I will." I reach for my phone, but—damn. It's not in my pocket. I always put it right back in my pocket after my shift, but I like to keep it...in my apron. It's hanging with my apron right now. "Shit, Cece, I left my phone at work. I'm going to run back and get it."

"I have to get back, too." Cece owns a pottery shop on Main Street, where you can paint your own plates and mugs and serving trays. "Text me!"

"I will."

Then she's moving again, a blur of blonde hair flying back toward the main drag. It's only a few seconds before she turns the corner. As soon as she's out of sight, I turn on my heel, ready to hustle back to the Short Stack.

But I'm stopped short, running straight into what feels like a wall of muscle.

Muscle...topped with frosting.

Chapter Ten

RYDER

I TAKE ONE STEP OUTSIDE THE BAKERY, STILL TRYING TO CLOSE the top of the cupcake container, when a woman whirls right into me, crushing two of them against my shirt.

"Oh, shit," she says, her hands going out to the smear of frosting.

Then her eyes go up to my face.

"Oh, shit, it's you," she breathes.

It's Valentine, but here in the afternoon sun, she's a different Valentine than the woman I snapped at during breakfast at the Short Stack two days ago.

It's only been two days, and I haven't stopped thinking about her. Last night, I finally forced myself to stop staring out the front window like some kind of stalker and go to bed, even though I'm dying to know just how close Valentine's house is to mine.

Would a summer fling be *so* bad?

She's wearing the same black T-shirt as before, but now I can see the jean shorts that hug the curves of her hips, and damn if she's not the most gorgeous woman on the planet.

"First whipped cream, and now this?" I say it like I'm a little bit pissed off, but I can't help grinning at her. I didn't mean to run into her like this. I'm not the kind of man who normally buys cupcakes at the bakery. But they're having a party at Minnie's brand-new daycare. We walked in the place an hour ago, just to check it out, and she fell in love with the toys, with the other children, with the kindly middle-aged woman, Norma, who owns the place. Minnie didn't want to leave, and I need to run some errands—namely, visit my brother. All Norma asked was that we bring a little something for the party since she'd only planned on so many kids.

So here I am, with cupcake frosting on my shirt and a pressing errand that I need to take care of.

"Now this," Valentine agrees, her eyes flicking over the mess on my shirt. Her expression changes, like she's made a decision. "I think the whipped cream might have been a better look."

I give her a hurt expression. "Better than this?"

She grins, opening her mouth to reply, but just then the bakery door opens and Leslie, the woman inside, is there holding another tray of cupcakes. "I saw what happened," she says. "Some replacements, on the house."

"You don't have to do that," I tell her, but she's already pressing the second tray into my hands—this one closed properly so no more accidents can happen. Then she's gone, leaving Valentine and I standing out on the sidewalk, looking after her. "Tell me it's not like this all the time."

"Like what?"

"Sweeter than sweet." I look back into Valentine's green eyes. "So sweet it's fucking disgusting."

Her mouth drops open a little, and then she laughs out loud. It's not a nervous laugh, it's full and pure, and I love the sound of it. "Sorry to disappoint, but that's Lakewood."

"Damn. I was hoping at least one person here wouldn't give me a canker sore from all the sugar."

Something has broken open between us, something has shifted in the air. I have to get back to that daycare, have to get back to the task at hand, but I don't want to move an inch. I don't want to shatter this moment.

"I'm not sweet," Valentine says abruptly.

That calls for some serious side-eye. "Oh, please. I saw you blushing all during breakfast at the Short Stack."

"Being a good waitress doesn't mean I'm like all of these people. Trust me." There's a defiance in her expression that makes me want to know more—makes me want to know everything.

"Yeah? How are you any different?"

"You're one to judge," she shoots back. "You live in a cottage by the lake, a cutesy place just like everybody else."

I pretend to be surprised. "Are you *stalking* me?"

She rolls her eyes. "I notice when someone moves in across the street, yes."

"You also told me about the place when you didn't have to." I lean a little closer and get a big breath of her scent. Judging by her outfit, she's been working at the Short Stack all morning, but underneath the smell of pancakes and bacon is something clean and pure and intoxicating. "It's almost like...you *wanted* me to move there."

The air between us goes as hot as Valentine's face. This is closer to flirting than we ever got during breakfast, not counting the whipped cream incident, and my mind screams a warning. *This is how you got fucked over in the first place.* I shove that thought out of my head. Not every single moment for the rest of my life has to be ruined by Angie. Only some of them.

Valentine's lips part, and damn if I don't want to wrap my hand around the back of her head and pull her in for a kiss right now. If I weren't holding these cupcakes... "That's ridiculous," she says, but I don't quite believe her. "I don't know anything about you."

"What more do you want to know? I'm an open book."

She laughs out loud again. "Ryder Harrison, you are the *least* open book ever to eat at the Short Stack."

"And yet we're already on a first-name last-name basis."

"If we're so close…" A playful look flashes across her face. "How come you haven't stopped over to say hello, like a good neighbor?"

"Whoever said I'd be a good neighbor? I won't even be in town that long."

"I'm hoping you'll be a bad one," Valentine says with a wicked look in her eyes, and the next moment her face is a deep red. But she doesn't look away from me. She *commits.* "You know, the kind of guy who…who's always mowing the lawn."

I raise my eyebrows. "Mowing the lawn?"

"Mowing the lawn." She's deadly serious. "Shirtless."

Chapter Eleven

VALENTINE

I HAVE NO IDEA HOW THAT CONVERSATION ENDED BECAUSE IN an attempt to protect me from literally dying of embarrassment, my brain blacked the entire thing out. All I know is three hours later, is that somehow I got to my car and drove home. I didn't even remember my phone, which was the entire reason I ran my awkward ass into Ryder in the first place.

I've been in the shower for a long time—I don't know how long—and no matter how cold the water gets, my cheeks still burn.

I told him I wanted him to mow the lawn shirtless. I told him that. *I spoke those words out loud with my mouth.*

Worst of all, it's true. I *do* want to see Ryder Harrison without his shirt on. I've wanted that from the moment I saw him at the Short Stack. What I don't want is to get attached, and get burned again, like with Conrad. God, that was a disaster...and all over something that turned out to be nothing.

But Ryder wouldn't be like that. Clearly.

Or maybe he would. I don't know. I don't know anything about him.

I step out of the shower, towel off, and throw on a tank and some shorts. I'm not going out again tonight. Tomorrow, Cece's made plans for us, but tonight I'm staying in with a good book.

I am *definitely* not going to stroll across the lawn to the other cottage. This property used to be two lots, back in the day, but the families who owned them had the same company build identical cottages on either end, with a wide lawn in the middle. My parents bought the lots as a kind of a package deal before I was born, and they only open the other building if they need the space. We're not the kind of family who loves reunions, so that's basically never. Thus, there is absolutely no reason for me to go walking out there. Not at all.

I've just settled in on the small screened-in porch facing the lake when I hear it.

The hum of a mower, coming from across the street.

* * *

I sit with the book open in my hands for a full five minutes, my heart practically beating out of my chest.

Ryder Harrison is baiting me.

I force my eyes back to the page. No. I'm not going to be baited. That was mortifying, what I said earlier, and what am I supposed to do now? Go over and look at him like he's a piece of man meat?

No. Absolutely not.

On the other hand...

I'm not going to be living here forever. And neither is he. I promised myself in the spring that I'd be out in a year, so at most, I'll only have to suffer through eight months of awkwardness.

I don't have to suffer at all if I just stay inside.

I bite my lip.

I have to know. That's the awful truth of it—I just have to know.

But *he* doesn't have to know.

I put the book on the table and stand up, adrenaline flooding my veins. I assess my outfit. It's fine for what I'm about to do.

I go out the front door of the cottage, scanning around the maple trees to see if he's in sight. The mower hums loudly, off to the left. He must be beside his own house. If I cut diagonally across the lawn, I'll be shielded by the hedge, then by the maple tree.

Halfway across the lawn I realize I'm *sneaking*, hunched over like a caricature of a robber. Yes, it's true, I am a grown woman. I straighten up, but I can't help walking softly...as if the sound of the lawnmower isn't going to cover up my approach over the *grass* on the other side of the street.

This is where I'm at now. I might as well embrace it. Worst-case scenario, he's wearing a shirt.

I come up behind the maple tree. It's huge, the trunk thick and round, and easily conceals me from the other side of the street. The only issue I face now is that it also conceals the other side of the street from me, so all I can hear is the damn mower.

It's quiet now, like he's behind the house, which is set back from the road by a stretch of yard. I bet Minnie would love a play-house out there. The Culvers never had kids, so there's nothing of the kind. Maybe I could—

I shake myself out of the weird plan I've started to make involving one of those playhouses that they sell in front of the hard-ware store when the sound of the mower gets louder.

I have to play this cool.

If he's coming toward the road, that means that eventually he'll turn back and face the house. *That* will be my moment. That'll be when I finally get a glimpse of those ripped shoulders.

Behind the tree, every fiber of my being is locked on listening to the sound of the mower. It gets louder and louder. I'm in tune with the sound; the sound is me. I hear the shift in the noise as he reaches the road, pushing the front of the mower a couple of inches onto the asphalt, and then I hear it as he turns back.

Heart in my throat, I move to the left side of the tree and lean out, ever so carefully.

He *is* shirtless.

"Damn," I whisper, because even his back is sexy.

Just then, a white stripped-down Jeep zooms down the road between us, and the group of college girls inside lets out a loud, uniform *whoop* that pierces air. "Ow ow ow!" one of them screams at the tail end, and that's probably what brings my plan crashing to a halt.

Ryder turns at the sound, but by the time he's facing the road again, the Jeep is gone. The sight of his absolutely fucking gorgeous body in the sun has addled my brain, and it's only at the last second that I jump back behind the tree.

I hold my breath.

He probably didn't see me. This tree is huge, and I've been careful to put it directly between me and his house. He probably—

The sound of the mower cuts off.

No. No no no no no. He's not going to catch me doing this. It's not going to happen. It can't happen. If it happens, I'll never live it down. I'll have to move, and I can't move. Not today, anyway.

I cross my fingers on both hands. No no no.

"Valentine?" His voice sends blood rocketing to my cheeks. I have to be redder than a stop sign. "Are you hiding behind that tree?"

Chapter Twelve

RYDER

I'M NOT A HUNDRED PERCENT SURE IT *IS* VALENTINE WHEN I call across the road. After all, it could be anyone with red hair like hers. All I saw was a ponytail as it flashed back behind the tree, and maybe an inch of the creamy skin of her forehead. But after that Jeep full of the kind of idiots I'm *not* interested in went by, I definitely saw movement behind one of the big maples across the road.

Okay. I lied. I *am* a hundred percent sure it's her. The only question now is whether she'll come out from behind the tree or run away from me again.

After she announced that she's interested in seeing me shirt-less and performing yardwork, the conversation totally petered out. Valentine stammered something about needing to get home and made a beeline around me.

I only realized I was standing there with a goofy smile on my face when the bakery door opened a second time, and there was Leslie, wanting to know if everything was all right with the cupcakes.

Yeah. Everything was. And things might be all right with the rest of my life, too. At least, I have the bizarre sensation that that's how they're heading, even if it all turns out to be shit in the end.

My brother wasn't home when I finally made it to his place after a quick stop at the daycare place and another one at the big box store south of town to buy a new package of T-shirts and a baby monitor that connects to my phone via an app. I can't say I'm disappointed, but I do still need to talk to him. I've been putting it off all week, and now that things are...different, I'm ready to get it over with.

But first, the lawn.

I swung by the daycare and picked up Minnie just before three, gave her a snack, and put her down in the Pack N' Play. I'm going to need a crib sooner or later, or maybe even an honest-to-god toddler bed. She was out in less than a minute. I plugged in the monitor and headed out to the shed in the back where Mrs. Culver had assured me I'd find all the tools required to keep up appearances on the house and lawn.

She wasn't lying. It was all gassed up and ready to go. I only hesitated for a second before stripping off my shirt and tossing it onto the porch on the first pass. My phone is set up to alert me if Minnie makes any noise, so it was the perfect time to call Miss I'm-Not-Sweet's bluff.

The first four passes across the yard—it's bigger than I thought—I saw no sign of her. I started to think maybe this was some kind of fucked-up hazing game, but Jesus, we're not in high school. No way.

Then I saw that flash of her hair.

"I saw you," I call out through the breeze.

A few more beats go by, and then Valentine steps out from behind the maple tree and gives me a sheepish wave. "Hey," she calls back.

"Are you done hiding behind the tree?"

"I wasn't hiding."

"Bullshit."

She covers her eyes with her hands like that will make this entire situation go away, then uncovers them. "This is your fault, you know."

"It's my fault that you were spying on me from behind a tree?"

She presses her lips into an embarrassed line. "I guess it's my fault."

"I'd say. You were the one who started all this, back at the bakery. I'm pretty sure you said—"

"Stop, stop!" She waves her hands in the air. "Everyone's going to hear you."

I shout louder. "Everyone's going to hear me say that you asked me to mow my lawn shirtless just so you could—"

Valentine looks both ways and then darts across the street, coming to a breathless halt in front of me. She looks so damn gorgeous, her damp hair in a braid over her shoulder, wearing a tiny pair of shorts and a tank top that stretches perfectly over her curves. Her eyes are bright and her cheeks are pink and even though I know I shouldn't mess with her—I shouldn't mess with anyone, I need to focus on building a new life from nothing—I can't help but fall a little bit. Just a little. "Stop. The entire neighborhood's going to hear you," she says in a voice just above a whisper.

"Why are you whispering?" There's a strip of trees on either side of the rental property, and she's the only one across the street.

She grins. "I don't want people to know."

"Know what? That you asked me to—" I'm having too much fun with this, and I know it.

"I didn't ask you to mow your lawn shirtless," she says, almost hissing the words. "I just *said* that I wouldn't mind if you were that kind of guy." Her gaze flicks over my shoulders, my abs.

"And then you ran away."

She goes an even deeper red. "I had somewhere to be."

"Yeah. Behind that tree, watching me mow my lawn."

"I just wanted to see if you'd...if you'd actually do it."

I raise my hands into the air at my sides. "I did."

"Why?" There's a sudden seriousness to her tone, even though she's still smiling.

"To make your dream come true." I mean to say it as a joke. It doesn't come off that way. The look in Valentine's eyes deepens, and she bites her lip.

"You think my only dream was to see you shirtless?" I think she means for it to come off like she's hardly dreamed of seeing me, but it doesn't sound like that. It doesn't sound like that at all.

"No. Just one of them." Her green eyes are blazing into my core. It might as well be a thousand degrees out here.

"You're right," she says, but there's a tremble in her voice. "I have *tons* of other dreams. And plans."

The urge to touch her rages out of control. It's been a long week. It's been a long two years. It's been a long *day,* for God's sake, and I give into that urge.

I reach out and brush my knuckles across the pink blush on her cheek. The contact is electric. It's all I can do not to take her in my arms right now, right here in the front yard. Valentine gasps at my touch.

"I'll make another one of your dreams come true." I drop my hand and step a little closer. Valentine's breasts rise and fall under her shirt, looking round and perfect as hell.

"How do you know what my—"

My phone goes off in my pocket, a loud chime.

"Shit. That's Minnie."

"Calling you?" Valentine's brow furrows.

"No, I have—" I dig the phone out of my pocket and swiped the screen to end the alert. Then I open up the monitor's app. There, on the screen, she's stirring in her Pack N' Play, her arms stretched over her head. "I have an app." Just then, the sound kicks in, and Minnie's sweet little voice comes over the phone's speakers.

"Hey, Daddy?" She yawns. "Hey, Daddy?"

I put the phone back in my pocket and meet Valentine's eyes. Hot *damn* do I wish I could stay here with her. Or invite her back in. But nap time is over. "I have to head in."

"Me too. I'll see you later," she says quickly, and before I can reach out and touch her again she's headed back across the road. I start dragging the lawnmower back to the shed. I can finish the lawn later. But I'm not done with Valentine, even if she's running away...again.

"Valentine!" I stop moving and call after her, loud and clear. She skids to a halt in the grass on the other side of the road.

"Yeah?" she shouts back.

"Go out with me."

A pause. "When?"

"Tomorrow night."

"I can't. I have plans."

"Saturday, then."

This is not how I envisioned planning my next date, in a shouted conversation across a street, but what the hell.

"Okay," Valentine shouts. Then she turns on her heel and sprints out of view.

Chapter Thirteen

VALENTINE

THINGS MIGHT NOT BE OFF TO THE MOST IMPRESSIVE START with Ryder, but if anything's going to make me feel good as hell about this, it's cocktails with Cece. After my shift at the Short Stack, I head back home. Ryder's car isn't in his driveway, and I feel a twinge of disappointment about it...but not enough to keep me from enjoying a too-long shower. At least I don't have to worry about him interrupting my extensive beauty routine for nights when I'm going out on the town. I spent fifteen minutes instead of my usual ten drying and straightening my hair.

Cece appreciates the effort, letting out a loud *whoop* when I slide into the booth across from her at the new wine bar in town.

Like all trendy new things that come to Lakewood, it'll be gone by next summer.

"Damn, girl," says Cece, raising her wine glass to her lips. "You look amazing."

"You started without me."

"Of course I did." She signals the waitress, who brings a second glass of Moscato. "I didn't want your wine to get warm, though. You can thank me later."

The instant the sweet wine hits my lips, I'm practically transported. It's chilled to perfection. Okay, maybe I was wrong. Maybe the wine bar will stick around.

Cece looks good, too, in what looks like her favorite little black dress. She always looks good. Cece is the kind of person who looks put together even when she's a hot mess. I can't even pretend to be anything other than a hot mess. "You're right," I tell her. "This is amazing."

She puts her glass down on the table. "I also...ordered appetizers."

"That's my girl."

"Speaking of my girl, are you doing okay?" The shift in conversation is so abrupt that I just blink at her for a moment. I didn't tell a single soul about the embarrassing encounter with Ryder yesterday, or about him renting the Culvers' house. Then it clicks. Once again, she's talking about Conrad.

I don't want to talk about Conrad, but Cece is on the hunt for more details. I never told her exactly *why* we broke up—I only sent her several increasingly mortifying texts—and I know she's dying to hash it out. I'm *more* interested in talking about Ryder, but talking about Ryder will mean admitting that I probably have a ridiculous crush on him.

Probably.

"Yeah," I say, rolling the stem of the wine glass between my fingers. "Yeah, I'm doing fine." The truth is that Ryder is the perfect distraction, even if a man like him could never be anything else.

"You don't want to talk about it."

"I really don't." I give her a wide grin, and Cece rolls her eyes.

"But I *really* want to know. I want to hear, in detail, exactly how that prick finally proved to you that he's an asshole."

My heart twists in my chest. It sucked what happened with Conrad. More than sucked. It ripped me apart, and not just because I thought I was in love with him. Maybe I really *was* in love with him, but even if that wasn't true, it was just another thing gone wrong in a string of things that didn't turn out.

I take another sip of the wine, steeling myself. This is the first sit-down I've had with Cece since everything happened. I should just get it over with.

"He broke up with me, for starters."

She cocks her head. "I'll wait."

"We broke up because..." I take a deep breath. Thinking

about it makes my stomach turn. I was scared, too, but Conrad...

"I guess things hadn't been going very well for a while."

"I'd say."

It's amazing how, now that we're not together, everyone in my life is willing to share opinions about Conrad. If they'd told me sooner that it would end like this, maybe I wouldn't have wasted so much time on him.

"You know, Cece, you could have mentioned something when we got together two years ago."

She just looks at me. "Did I really have to mention it? Out loud? With words?"

I look down into my wine. It's true. Just after Conrad and I started dating seriously, I brought him home to spend the Fourth of July at Lakewood. He was his usual self — focused on having a good time. Now that I look back, he was *only* interested in having a good time, even if it meant being an asshole to everyone else, including me. Sharon hadn't liked him, either. My mother was not a fan. And Cece...of course she hated him. I chalked it up to the heat, why everyone seemed to be in an edgy mood.

"No. I guess not."

Cece's expression is somewhere between sympathy and serious. I can't just *not* tell her. "What happened, Val? You said you'd never come back to Lakewood."

That makes me laugh. "I said a lot of things when I was eighteen."

"You meant it, though."

"Fine." I sigh. "Things came to a head a couple months ago." It makes my throat tight to say this. "I had a..." I can't find the words, but Cece waits. "I had thought I might be pregnant."

Her mouth drops open. "Oh, my God, Val, but—"

"I wasn't." I rush the words out before she gets any other ideas. "I was just...late by a few days. I don't know what happened. Stress, maybe, from the job?" I'd *had* an entry-level job at a more prestigious marketing firm in the city, but the pay was shit and the hours were way longer than any shift I'd worked at the Short Stack. "But Conrad lost his mind. He completely shut down." His words had been like acid arrows, and it makes me flinch just to think of the conversation we had after I told him I was worried. I let out a bitter laugh. "He was so damn relieved when I got my period."

"And then he kicked you out?"

"Not right then. About a week later. I got home from work one day, and he was waiting there to tell me it just wasn't going to work out. The pregnancy scare had made him realize that he didn't want to be with me."

Cece's lips are curled in disgust. "What a bastard. After four years. Jesus."

"That's when I texted you." She nods. "I got a different place and tried to make it work, but..." I let my voice trail off. The rent had been too damn high. The rent, the bills—Conrad had mostly taken care of those kinds of things. He never had to worry about money. "I quit my job two weeks ago and moved back the same day. I just need to..." I don't know what the hell I need to do. "I just need some time, I guess. Then I'll be on my way."

"You could just stay, you know." Cece grins. "I missed you."

Could I? I don't know. It didn't seem like there was much for me in this place when I graduated high school and headed to college. It still doesn't. But at least I have a friend. And what the hell else do I have to lose? Nothing.

I don't have *anything* to lose.

It makes me think of Ryder. Excitement spikes out from my chest.

"Whoa," says Cece. "What are you thinking about? You look like you just remembered something sexy."

"I'll never tell."

"Yes, you *will*." Cece leans forward, eyes bright. "Tell me. Tell me right now."

Part of me wants to tell her, but another part hesitates. He's got a daughter, for God's sake. I'm clearly not cut out for any of that, even if he *was* interested in something more than a few dates, a fling. I'm sure he's not. I'm sure of it.

I give Cece a coy look and order more wine instead.

Chapter Fourteen

RYDER

"**C**OME IN!"
The sound of my brother's voice takes me totally aback. For once, he doesn't sound pissed off, ready to come after me with swinging fists. And to think he was a nerd in high school. Back then, he never would have raised a hand to anybody. It's not like he's ever actually punched me, I guess, but when I joined the Army two weeks after graduation, he was the most irate I've ever seen him. Looking back, maybe it was fear that made him so pissed off.

The week before I left was a tense one, to say the least.

"Hello!" Minnie calls the word from her spot in my arms, waving merrily even though I haven't opened the door yet.

"Wait a second, sweetheart," I tell her, then take a deep breath and open the door.

We step into the foyer of exactly the kind of house I'd always expected my brother to own: big and tidy and everything in neutral shades. Somewhere, I guarantee it, he's got an office with one of those computers with three separate monitors or some shit like that. It's probably in the basement.

"I'm in the kitchen. You can come on back."

I shouldn't be this nervous to see him, but it's been a few years, and things have obviously changed. I follow the sound of his voice down a hallway with hardwood floors—nice as fuck—and into a wide, bright kitchen. My brother, skinnier than me with dark hair, stands at the sink. His hands work over a carrot he's peeling, one of those thick orange ones that's clearly from the farmer's market.

Lakewood *would* have a farmer's market.

"Say 'Hello, Uncle Jamie,'" I tell Minnie.

"Hi, Uncle Jamie," she says, looking shy, pulling her baby doll closer in.

My brother takes a deep breath and sets the peeler down in the sink alongside the carrot, then turns. For all our differences, he has the same eyes as I do. And Minnie.

"Hey, squirt," he says, and then he can't help himself. He grins at her, and she gives him her biggest toddler smile. Nobody can help themselves around Minnie. "Nice to meet you. Finally."

It's a jab at me, but a pretty mild one, considering.

I look him in the eye, the three of us standing there in silence. Well, screw that. I've got limited time here, and Jamie was never the enemy. "Hey."

"Hey," he says back, sticking his hands in his pockets.

"About leaving town without warning you..."

He wrinkles his forehead. "Are you talking about six years ago?"

"Yeah. About that—"

"That was a total di—" Minnie is still grinning at him, and he cuts himself off abruptly. "That—that was a silly thing to do."

"The *silliest* thing to do," I echo him.

"Silly," says Minnie solemnly.

"I'm sorry."

Jamie scowls at me for a split second, but Minnie is just too damn cute. "You missed out on a lot."

"Like what?"

"Jamie, who are these lovely people?" The voice singing out from behind us is somehow familiar, but I can't place it until she flits by me, moving across the kitchen and planting a kiss on Jamie's cheek. Then she laughs like this is all some kind of wonderful joke. "Ryder! Jamie didn't say you were coming to visit."

I gape at her, my mouth hanging open.

"Hi!" Minnie says, waving.

"Hi, sweetheart! What's your name?"

"I'm Minnie!" says Minnie, and immediately starts squirming to get out of my arms. "Minnie!"

I finally break out of my own stunned silence. "Poppy Harwood, what are you doing with my brother?" Yes, she kissed him on the cheek, but there's no way. There's no *way* that he and Poppy Harwood, the queen of his class in high school, are—

She laughs, flipping her blonde hair over her shoulder, and crouches down. Minnie untangles herself from my arms and goes shyly over to her, tentatively holding out her baby doll. "Baby doll," she says, and then pushes it out another two inches.

Poppy claps one hand to her chest and reaches out to take the doll, still holding it within Minnie's reach. "Oh, she's *beautiful*," she says. "What's her name?"

"It's a baby doll," says Minnie.

I have to go back to my brother on this because I *have* to know how he landed the most popular girl in his class — no, the entire school. Nobody was on a higher tier than Poppy Harwood. Homecoming Queen. Prom Queen. All that shit, and then amplified a thousand times over. And here she is, fawning over Minnie's doll like she's just a regular person.

Living with my brother, like he's not the most regular nerd you've ever met in your life.

He glances down at the pair of them and then turns back

to the sink. The carrot and the peeler are out in a flash and on a clean paper towel next to the sink, and then he's reaching into the fridge for a couple of beers.

No formal invitation needed. I'm in.

It feels almost normal following him out to the back deck. It feels almost right. I'll miss this at the end of the summer when I leave.

The patio has a furniture set — a real, honest-to-god set of patio furniture — and we both take seats. Open beers. Look at each other one more time.

"You have patio furniture, Jamie. What else have I missed?"

"Poppy, for one," he says with a satisfied little smile that I've never seen on his face before.

"You guys married?"

He rolls his eyes. "No, asshat. I didn't marry her without telling you."

"You could have."

"You'd have deserved it." He's damn right, too. I didn't tell him — or my parents — that Angie was pregnant until Minnie was born. I was that fucking ashamed of the whole thing. Not Minnie herself — I could never be ashamed of her. But Angie — shit. That was a disaster from the very beginning.

"I know." The words practically choke me, but it's now or never. "I'm sorry."

Jamie leans back with a nod and takes a swig of his beer. "So what the hell happened to you?"

How can I explain it to him? I graduated by the skin of my damn teeth, and the Army seemed like a way out of the town we'd grown up in. Southeast Michigan had nothing to offer me. War seemed like some grand adventure. And after I learned it wasn't, *Angie* seemed like a grand adventure. I didn't realize until it was too late that she was more of a suicide mission.

I want to tell him everything, but I can hear Minnie's voice. She's giggling, and I just can't get into it now. Not when she could come bursting out here at any second.

"It all went wrong," I say.

Jamie's eyes narrow, but he doesn't press me. He was furious when I left home. *Furious.* But maybe I've been seeing it all wrong. Maybe it's the years since then that have been the worst for him. They were for me, damn it.

"Lakewood's nice," he says into the silence.

"Yeah." I look out over his lawn, at the ring of trees surrounding it that bleed into the forest behind. "I probably won't stay long."

"No?"

"Just the summer. I rented a place through August."

"So you're just passing through?"

I open my mouth, and an image of Valentine's cheeks,

blushing pink, pops into my head. "Just passing through," I tell him, but even I'm not totally convinced.

Another swig of beer glides down my throat, and Poppy's voice floats out the window, singing Itsy Bitsy Spider. Minnie is beside herself with laughter and then joins in, her little voice high and pure. I lock eyes with my brother. "Jamie."

He gives me a wary look.

"What?"

"I have to ask you a favor."

Chapter Fifteen

VALENTINE

IT ONLY OCCURS TO ME AFTER I'VE ALREADY PICKED OUT THE shorts that make my ass looked the best, my very best halter top waiting for me on my bed for the last possible moment, and spent forty minutes on my makeup and hair that we never set a time for our date.

We. Never. Set. A. Time.

I gasp out loud and send my hair straightener clattering to the tile floor in the attempt to snatch my phone from the bathroom counter.

But the phone does me absolutely no good because I don't have Ryder's number. And why *would* I have Ryder's number? No reason at all, except I stalked him into going on a date with me, and now I have no choice but to...

...but to what? Awkwardly knock on his door, dressed to the nines—at least as far as Lakewood going-out attire goes—and see if he still wants to go out with me? He didn't come to the Short Stack during my shift yesterday, damn it, and that's a real loss because not only did I not get to look at him and flirt with him to redeem myself after the whole hiding-behind-a-tree-and-running-away-afterward incident, I didn't get to confirm our plans.

If I just stay in my house and pretend not to exist, at least he won't know that I spent all this time dressing up for him.

What time is it, even?

Close to seven. *Date time.*

I scroll through my contacts list just in case he somehow slipped it into my phone when I was busy embarrassing myself. No luck.

Well, there's no reason to leave things in disarray just because I couldn't remember to *exchange phone numbers* with the guy I'm supposed to be going out with at some point tonight.

That is, if the entire thing wasn't just a funny joke. Because what man who looks like Ryder is going to go on a *date* with a woman who hid behind a tree just to look at his glorious body in the sunlight?

And shit, it *is* glorious. A thousand times hotter than any man I ever laid eyes on in college. A million times hotter than anyone currently in Lakewood. God help me, I want to do all sorts of dirty, filthy things with...

The knock at the door jerks me right out of an extended fantasy involving a solid wood headboard, my knuckles white against the wood, holding on for dear life as Ryder takes me from behind, his hands on my waist. The straightener, which I meant to put away several minutes ago, is still clutched in my hands, a poor substitute for that headboard.

Someone knocking at the door. Right.

I place the straightener delicately in its drawer and force myself not to hesitate at all on the way through the cottage. Damn my parents for replacing the glassed-in door with one that's solid wood—well, maybe not *solid,* nothing like that imaginary headboard. I pull it open standing tall, hoping I look at least slightly radiant. This is my chance to show him a different me.

Ryder is standing on the other side of the storm door, and when he sees me, a grin spreads across his face, slow and hot and so sultry I could die. Maybe it doesn't matter after all that we never set a time. He's clearly interested, or he wouldn't be standing here right now. And even if it's just for one date, the pride swelling in my chest is a salve on the wound that Conrad slashed into my heart.

"Hey," I say, feeling my face stretch into an echoing grin. Holy *shit,* he's hot, even with a shirt on—a plain black t-shirt that still somehow manages to look dressy. Like they always say, sometimes it's the hanger that makes the outfit. Or something like that. Not that Ryder is a hanger. Not anywhere close.

"Hi, Valentine," he says, those blues electric on mine.

"I was— " I swallow hard. "I was just thinking that we never set a time, and I don't have your number, so—" *So maybe we should just call the whole thing off, and you could come in, and we could spend some time—*I laugh out loud at the thought of saying that to him, then cover it with what I hope is the world's sexiest smile. "I'm glad you remembered."

"There's no way I could forget you." Ryder's smile is hotter by the second.

I roll my eyes, feeling the heat flood my cheeks. "I did hide behind a tree. Let's just get that out into the open."

He laughs out loud, the sound sending waves of heat down my spine even through the glass pane of the storm door. "You seem to have recovered your confidence."

I stand up straighter. "Thank you. I have." I want to open the door, take his hand, and pull him inside. Then we can let whatever happens happen, even if it's right on the floor of the cottage's living room, on the rag rug my grandma made a zillion years ago. But this is a first date. We can't just— "You seem to be ready to go. Lakewood has *two* bars to choose from so it could be a wild night."

Ryder laughs again, and I bend to the table, drop my phone into my purse, and pick it up.

I have the storm door open when he stops me. "Valentine—"

"What?" I'm going to flirt with this man, come hell or high water. I've already made enough of a fool of myself. Tonight is going to be different. "Did you change your mind? We could always go back inside."

"I think you probably should." His eyes are glowing, and I just *barely* keep my jaw from dropping to the ground.

"Oh, yeah? Is that what you want to do?" Hot *damn* I am in my element.

Am I imagining it, or is there a little blush in his cheeks? That would be too much. Me, Valentine Carr, making a man like Ryder *blush*?

"I can come if you want to, but I think—" He sticks his hands in his pockets, and all it does is accentuate his ripped arm muscles.

"Tell me." I've dropped my voice into the flirtiest possible tone.

"I think you might want a moment to yourself, just to finish—you know, getting ready."

It brings me up short. A moment to myself? I don't need a moment to myself. The entire point of this was to get him to come in with me.

At that exact moment, a summer breeze kicks up caressing the bare skin of my stomach.

Of my *stomach.*

89

Which then plummets straight to the earth, because I'm not wearing my halter top. I'm standing just outside the door with a black, lacy, strapless bra on, telling Ryder that I'm ready to go out on a date.

I'm still frozen, hoping this is all some kind of nightmare, when Ryder follows it up like I might not have gotten it yet. "I think you forgot to put your shirt on, Valentine."

I could die.

Chapter Sixteen

RYDER

I DON'T KNOW THAT I'VE BEEN SO TORN IN MY LIFE AT THE moment Valentine opens the door and stands right there in shorts that are just long enough to qualify as decent and just short enough to make me want to tear them right off of her...and a black bra that looks like a sex wizard whipped it up out of some kind of special lace that makes me hard. Instantly.

Or maybe it's the way it wraps under her gorgeous breasts, lifting them *just so*.

I think it might be one of those sexy approaches to dating that isn't really dating until the moment I realize that Valentine doesn't know she's forgotten her shirt. And that moment is when she opens the door and steps toward me, all ready to head out to

AMELIA WILDE

whatever shitty restaurant we'll agree on in the car. If Lakewood even has restaurants, beyond the Short Stack. It must. Right?

But food is the last thing on my mind. Valentine looks fucking gorgeous. Her hair is shining, loose around her face, falling in liquid waves over her shoulders, and she's done whatever makeup tricks women do that make her look like a sexy nighttime version of herself.

I almost fucking blow it.

I see her catching on, see her feeling the breeze against her skin while I'm trying to hint to her that she *maybe forgot her shirt* and, fuck, I wouldn't mind if she just stripped off the rest of those clothes, too. Then, because I'm an idiot, and I'm a little struck by how good she looks right in this moment, in the summer evening sunlight, I spell it out for her.

Valentine's face goes a rosy scarlet color and my cock twitches against the fabric of my boxers. I want her right now and damn the consequences. Damn the fact that I don't have time to fall for a woman like Valentine. Damn the fact that I'm sure that if I take her, she'll always have a hold on me.

She looks up at me, biting her lip.

I expect her to turn around, go back through the door, and shut it tightly behind her. I brace myself to coax her out of there because this is embarrassing as fuck and both of us know it. Something inside me twists. I don't want to spend time convincing anyone to do anything. I'm out without Minnie for the first time in months, about to spend time with Valentine Carr, who looks like she walked out of my latest fantasies, and I don't want to waste a moment of it—

"I don't need a moment."

"You don't what?" The sight of her erases everything from my mind except the gentle line of her curves, and the way she'd look if she turned around and—

"I don't need a moment to myself." Well, I'll be damned. Valentine cracks a smile that makes me believe she's not totally mortified. Almost. "You can come in with me."

"Oh, I don't want to—" I raise my hands in front of me. To go inside Valentine's cottage would be a colossal fucking mistake. I can't afford to be distracted by her, behind solid walls, away from prying eyes, where we could—

"You're *not* intruding," she says, and grabs my hand, turning determinedly back into the house and tugging me along with her. "I'm inviting you."

"That's brave. What if I'm some kind of serial killer?"

We've stepped over the threshold, the storm door swinging shut behind us. Valentine drops my hand, but not before she gives it the faintest squeeze like she almost can't bear to let go. She crosses her arms over her chest and rolls her eyes. "A serial killer who takes cupcakes to his daughter's daycare? I don't think so."

I laugh. She can't stop herself from falling all over me. It's been a long time since I felt like this, and right then, something switches gears at my fucking core.

I can have whatever I want with Valentine. I'm leaving at the end of the summer anyway, and I want her. I want her so badly that I'm not going to let Angie ruin this for me. Not even the specter of Angie. Not a chance.

And Valentine is radiating heat. She hasn't made a single move toward her bedroom, or wherever the mysteriously missing shirt is. She just stands in the living area we've stepped into, head held high, chin up.

"Sorry," I say, finally. "What were we talking about?"

"You were just telling me how you're definitely *not* a serial killer."

"Yes. Yep. Not a serial killer."

She cocks her head to the side. "Is something on your mind?" The confidence in her face flickers. "You know, we don't have to do this if you have other plans. I know you have..." she pauses, searching for the words. "I know you have a lot to take care of."

I take a step toward her, closing the distance between us. "Valentine."

She sucks in a breath. "Yeah?"

"There is no way on *earth* I could be thinking of anything but you. You're standing here in nothing but a bra and shorts, and you look so fucking gorgeous that it's making me crazy."

It's Valentine who throws her arms around my neck, crashing into me so hard that our teeth click together. "Oh, *fuck*." She starts to pull away. "I can't believe that I—"

"It's like *this*." I pull her wrists gently behind my neck and slide one hand down the side of her waist. Her skin is so soft that I could do this for days, but I don't have that kind of time. I *do* have time to press her up against the wall, right next to the little table with her purse on it and raise my other hand to her jaw.

She gives a little sigh when I wrap my hand around her jawline and tilt her face up toward mine, lowering my head to bring our lips together *without* another collision.

Holy fuck, she tastes good. Sweet and minty, like her toothpaste, but there's another taste there that's all her. Valentine's lips part to let my tongue into her mouth and she moans into mine, just a little, just a tiny bit out of control.

I kiss her like I've never kissed anyone.

It's a long time before we come up for air.

But when we do, she pushes me back, gasping, cheeks pink, eyes shining.

"Was that okay?"

"*Okay?*" she practically screeches the word and then claps her hand over her mouth. "That was unbelievable. I..." Valentine shakes her head. "I have no words."

Is this happening right now? Are we about to go back to her bedroom so I can have my way with her?

But before I can open my mouth, she continues. "I have no words, except..." Then her expression turns sincere. "That I'm hungry."

"*Hungry?*"

"Starving."

I step close and whisper the words into her ear. "For love?"

She turns her head and whispers back. "For tacos." Then she whirls away, heading for what I assume is her bedroom. "Let's do that first, and then we can talk about love."

Chapter Seventeen

VALENTINE

KISSING RYDER IS LIKE BEING RIGHT IN THE CENTER OF A TWO-person fireworks show that begins somewhere in my chest and explodes out all the way to my fingertips. He is *not* an amateur. No. Not in the least. The sure, almost rough way he kisses me, pressing me back against the wall, the wood cool on my skin, has me soaked. There are no two ways about it.

My entire body aches to brace against him, my arms on his hard shoulders, and throw my legs around his waist. But there's a warning in the back of my mind that just won't let me do it. It's all happening so fast, and the heat between us is so intense, that it takes my breath away. He's dangerous, Ryder—he's not a safe bet. And I want that. I want that so much, that risky pleasure.

But I'm still wounded, and you know what they say about staying out of the kitchen.

When we come up for air I want to dive right back under, but instead, I throw my guard up, just a little bit.

Tacos.

Somehow I manage to string together several words relating to tacos and then sashay away from him toward my bedroom. All of me is trembling. I don't look back, but I think he must be watching me go.

He *is* watching me go, and there's a taut moment of silence.

Then he laughs.

It's not a cruel laugh like Conrad's. It's hot and surprised, astonished, even, and there's a delight in the sound that I wasn't expecting at all. I'm melting into a puddle of sheer desire, but to submerge myself right now wouldn't be...it wouldn't be...

I move through the door to my bedroom, snatch up the halter top from the bedspread, and put it on while Ryder is still laughing. "I get it, I get it," he calls, his voice moving down the hallway. "You want a *real* date."

I poke my head back out the door. "Just because I didn't have a shirt on doesn't mean I'm a loose woman." Not that I care what people do. Sex on the first date? With Ryder, it might be a foregone conclusion. Just not sex within the first *hour* of the first date.

"I never thought you were." His grin is so wicked that I almost cover my face with my hands so that he can't see how much it turns me on. "So, where's this Mexican place?"

"It's a little bit of a drive," I admit. Lakewood doesn't technically have a Mexican restaurant. You have to drive to the next town over to get something other than the homegrown American menus that are all over Main Street. There's a certain charm to independent restaurants, but that's not what I want right now.

"That's *terrible*," Ryder says as I make my way back down the hall, picking up my purse again. "Having to sit next to *you* while I drive us to the tacos you're demanding? I don't know how I'll stand it." For as tense as he seemed in the Short Stack, he's doing a shitty job pulling off authentic sarcasm. My heart beats faster.

"It's the price you'll have to pay." I pull the door closed behind us, not bothering to lock it. This is Lakewood, after all.

"Terrible," he repeats.

Then he reaches out, taking my hand in his.

* * *

I look at Ryder over the basket of tortilla chips, hot from under the warming lights. Watching him scoop them into the basket was somehow sexy. Maybe it's just the way his muscles flexed in the glow of those lights, but I could hardly stop myself from reaching out and raking my nails over his just-exposed bicep.

"We're on borrowed time," he says, popping a chip into his mouth. Jesus, even watching him *eat tortilla chips* is sexy.

"We are." I nod sagely. "We all are. It's true."

He laughs. "Not like that. I only have a sitter for a couple of hours, and we spent..." Ryder glances around at the clock shaped like a sombrero off to the side of our booth. "Fifteen minutes driving here."

"Oh, shit. Right. I...forgot about that." Could I *say* anything more cringeworthy than referring to his daughter as *that*?

Ryder's shoulders tense, just a little, but he seems to consciously relax them. "It's an easy thing to forget when you're in the presence of greatness."

He's willing to give me a pass this time. "It must be hard for you to remember *anything* right now." I reach for a chip and then dip it into the mild salsa.

"Oh, no. I'm not like that." His eyes are so blue it's hard to look at him, but I can't look away. "All of this is being burned into my memory."

As he says the words, I bite down hard, the chip crunching deliciously in my mouth.

The next moment is when the heat from the salsa blasts over my tongue. It's so hot that I gasp, which only fans the flames. "Oh, my *shit*," I shout around the mouthful. I can't swallow it—it's that intensely hot, but I can't spit it out on the table. What the hell is this salsa? It's not the garden salsa that I *thought* I was biting into.

Ryder leans forward, half out of his seat. "Are you okay? What's going on? Are you allergic to something?"

What do I do? *Whatdoldo?*

I reach for my water glass, then for a napkin, then just fan uselessly at my mouth. "The salsa—"

Behind Ryder, in the distance, I see our waitress turn, register how ridiculous I look, and start to hurry over. No. The *last* thing I need is a bigger audience.

I grab up the water glass and force myself to take a big sip, washing down the remnants of chip and salsa. It does nothing to quench the heat. The only option is to take another chip and shove it into my mouth. It's salty as hell, but at least it's not salsa. My eyes are watering.

"I am *so* sorry," our waitress—her nametag reads *Jennifer*—says as she rushes up to the table. She can't be much older than seventeen if that. "I must have taken that from the wrong..." She trails off and watches me take a second chip, then a third, chewing them as fast as I possibly can. "I'm so sorry." She lifts the offending salsa from the table but then has nowhere to put it, so she just stands there holding it in her hand.

"It's all right," Ryder says, standing up from his seat and throwing his arm out like this waitress might attack us both. "I've got this."

I swallow the chips as he moves purposefully around the table, sliding into the booth next to me and wrapping me up in one

101

strong arm. *Oh, my God.* Then he's lifting my chin with two fingers, not unlike he's about to do mouth-to-mouth, and covers my mouth with his. Only it's *not* like mouth-to-mouth. It's another kiss as charged as the one back at the cottage.

He kisses me so deeply that the waitress blushes, then spins on her heel and makes a beeline for the kitchen. I only see it because I'm desperate to know if everyone in this restaurant is staring at us, and then I'm lost again, swept away by the feel of his lips against mine.

Ryder pulls back abruptly, his eyes...not quite concerned. "Is that better?" His tone is urgent, but there's something else there, too.

I raise a hand to my lips, breathing hard. "You're laughing at me."

"Absolutely not." He can't even keep the smile off of his face. He's biting his lip, like that's going to hide that grin.

"You are *laughing* at me." My tongue is on fire—still—but I'm smiling back at him in spite of myself.

"I've never seen anyone react that way to salsa." He shakes his head solemnly. "It was bad enough that I wasn't sure you were going to make it." How is it this is sexy, that he's teasing me? How is it somehow fine that he kissed me like that, even if it's *supposed* to be a joke?

"It wasn't normal salsa!" I shout, and heads turn at the nearby tables. "That was mango habanero salsa. It's a special here." I lower my voice and hiss the last phrase at him. "It's unbelievably hot."

Ryder lets go of me and crosses his arms over his chest. "Hotter than me?"

I cross my own arms. "What's your game, Ryder Harrison? Do you always need this many compliments?" I'm in awe of myself, just a little, for being able to get these sentences together with my scorched tongue.

"Oh, no," he says, his voice catching at my core. "I need a lot more than that."

Chapter Eighteen

RYDER

"**H**OW COULD YOU POSSIBLY NEED MORE THAN THAT?" Valentine swallows again, breathing slowly. I don't know what was in that salsa, but I want some. But not as much as I want another excuse to kiss her. I know we're doing this all wrong—I should be staying away from her, or at least taking this at a glacial pace—but I can't help myself. The way her eyes are dancing in the dim light of this Mexican restaurant is pulling me in.

"A man has needs."

She rolls her eyes. It's a joke, and I'm glad she's taking it as one because I'm not buying her tacos so she'll have sex with me. I'm buying her tacos, *and* I think she wants to have sex with me, too—at least, that's how it feels when her luscious lips move against mine. And they are *damn* luscious. So luscious that it almost makes me forget that this is a huge risk I'm taking.

Almost, but not quite.

Jennifer the Waitress reappears with a tray heaping with food, still apologizing. "I'm so sorry about that salsa," she says.

I tear myself away from Valentine and go back to my own seat across the booth. "I'm not sorry." When I say it, I look at Valentine. She smiles, glancing down at her lap for a split second before Jennifer slides her plate in front of her. Within thirty seconds, we're alone again, and Valentine's expression has turned serious.

"I don't know why," she says, her tone thoughtful, "but I like you."

"I don't know why I like you, either. Maybe it's your incredible waitressing skills. You would *never* have brought the wrong salsa."

"Oh, *hell* no," says Valentine. "I'd never even touch that stuff. Although...that would probably get me fired from this place." She shrugs. "But that's okay. My job at the Short Stack was meant to be." She says the last few words with just a hint of sarcasm.

"Why isn't it meant to be?"

She pulls a tiny Mexican flag out of one of her tacos. "Are you sure you really want to get into the deep stuff right now?"

Under any other circumstances, I'd already be out the door of this restaurant and fifteen miles away. I haven't bothered to have a real conversation with anyone since what happened with Angie. I sigh a little bit, and Valentine smiles. She must already be anticipating another joke. Me, the guy with the light sense of humor—is that who I am now? "I don't mind if I'm getting deep into *you*."

It's probably the truest thing I've ever heard because I'm still painfully hard from kissing Valentine, tasting the sweetness of her lips. I'd like to taste the rest of her, too. She blushes. "Deep into my feelings, you mean?"

"Yes. Your *feelings*." I don't want to come off like a total ass-hole. "I mean, your feelings are really important to talk about."

Valentine shakes her head. "It's okay that you just want to get into my pants." Then she leans forward, blushing before she even says the words. "I'm willing to admit that I want you in my pants."

I laugh out loud. "You're a constant surprise."

"Why? Other women don't say that kind of thing to you?"

"Not normally. And not—"

Valentine primps her hair. "Not women who look like me? All innocent and waitress-y?"

"You got it. But I don't just want to get in your pants."

"No, you do, and that's okay." Valentine's green eyes are locked on mine. "A summer fling, right? Listen, I think we both know that we've got a *connection*." She drops her voice, her eyes crinkling with her smile. "But we don't have to pretend we're falling in love." She lifts a taco from her plate and holds it up like she's toasting me. "To tacos and sex!"

I didn't order tacos, but I hoist my burrito off of my plate, the sauce dripping onto my fingers. "Tacos and sex!"

But even as we both dissolve into laughter, I can't escape a tiny, sinking feeling.

* * *

"...so I came back here, and Sharon gave me my old job back. It's definitely..." Valentine pauses and eats another bite of taco while she thinks. "It's not terrible, but it's not what I had in mind for a post-college gig."

"I don't believe you."

"Which part?" She's been telling me about what brought her to Lakewood. We're racing against time for our date, and even though we toasted to tacos and sex and no commitments, Valentine still wants to play the dating game. I want to know about her, too. I've wanted to know more about her since the moment I saw her. "You have to believe she gave me my job back. We met at the Short Stack."

The more she tells me, the less I'll have to tell her about myself.

"I'll *never* forget meeting you at the Short Stack." I watch the color rise to her cheeks again. Valentine loves it when I drop my voice into that ever-so-slightly deeper tone. Her tell is her bright red cheeks. "But I don't believe that you, Valentine Carr, couldn't get a job at a marketing firm."

"Oh, I got a job." She eats some Spanish rice, and then a long drink of Diet Coke. "It's just that after the breakup, it was hard to find another one."

"Why would breaking up with that douchebag affect your job?" The second the words are out of my mouth, I feel like a complete dick. Who knows? Maybe she was such a wreck that she couldn't work. If it weren't for Minnie, I'd be a wreck right now, just from the stress. "I mean—"

Valentine grimaces. "It was owned by Conrad's dad, and he didn't...paint a very flattering picture of me. And somehow that information got to my manager, and then—" She rolls her eyes even harder. "The details aren't so important."

"Couldn't you sue the fuck out of them for that?"

"Probably, but who has time when there are pancakes to serve?" The nervous smile flashing across her face tells me that she's not thinking about that now, that she's still smarting from the wound. "Anyway, I put in for a few other jobs before I left the city, but I only have college references now. I can't use my manager at that firm." Her expression darkens. "Conrad really fucked things up for me. I just need a little while to regroup, and then I'm sure it'll be different."

It's already different for me. She's like a seismic shift,

something that changes the world forever, even if we can't go in for more than a summer fling. "I'm sure."

"So why are you in Lakewood?"

"My brother's here."

"That's the only reason?"

"Wouldn't you move to live near your sister?"

"No!" Valentine laughs. "I love her, but she does her own thing. And California is too far away."

"From what?"

"From you, for one thing." Valentine has to be joking, and she follows it up with a laugh. "I don't know. From the city?"

"I know how much you'd miss *the city*," I say meaningfully, raising one eyebrow. "You can admit that you have an enormous crush on me, Valentine. We've already kissed twice."

She straightens her back, trying to look prim. "Yes, and that was a mistake. We should be taking things slow."

I'm out of my seat in an instant, sliding into the booth next to her again. "Taking things *slow*?" Valentine's eyes go wide, and she draws in a big breath. "You just toasted me with a taco and told me this was about sex and Mexican food. A *summer fling*, is what you said. Summer flings aren't slow. Summer flings are fast and hot and spicy. Almost too spicy. So spicy they burn your mouth." Valentine bites her lip, and I lean down and kiss her just once, a glancing heat against my own lips. I lower my voice like this is the most important thing I'll ever say. And fuck, maybe it is. "If you don't want a summer fling, you can say so right now, Valentine. But if you do? It'll be so hot you'll never be the same. The things I want to do to you—" My cock pulses against my pants. Valentine's breathing hard. "We can have something that's too hot to last. Do you want that?" I run my fingers down the line of her jaw. "Tell me."

"I want that." Her voice is a sultry whisper. "When can we start?"

I lean down until my lips are barely an inch from her mouth and whisper, "As soon as you're finished with your tacos."

Valentine laughs, slapping at my shoulder. "Deal." Then she signals for the waitress. Jennifer scurries over. "I'm going to need a couple of boxes, Jennifer," Valentine says with a big smile. "We have to go."

Chapter Nineteen

VALENTINE

I'M TORN BETWEEN LAUGHING FOREVER AT THE FACT THAT we've both just agreed to a summer fling *so spicy it burns your mouth* and wanting to straddle Ryder in the front of his car.

I'd settle for holding his hand. Is that too relationship-y? Is that not appropriate summer fling behavior?

"What are you staring at? Do you not trust my driving skills?"

You know, if there's ever a time for radical honesty, it's during a summer fling. Time is short. I'm just going to tell him the damn truth. "I was looking at your hands."

"These sexy hands?" He takes them both off the wheel and holds them up.

"You're driving the car, Ryder! Get your hands back on the wheel!"

"I'd rather have my hands elsewhere."

"I will hold one of them, I *guess*." I pretend to be considering this for the first time. "Unless holding hands isn't what you do during a summer fling. I'm not an expert at this."

"I've only had one other fling," Ryder says, and something dark flits across his expression. "But I say, the fuck with the rules."

"The fuck with them."

"The only rule is that it's a fling." His tone is light, but he glances across at me, his gaze lingering just a second.

"Just a fling," I echo, and then I reach across, take his hand, and thread my fingers through it. It just feels so *right*. And if his hand feels good, then his cock....

Well, there's only one way to find out about that.

We fly through downtown Lakewood and take the highway back toward our places. My heart pounds. My place or his? My bed or his? Or not even a bed? Maybe just the floor? I'd fuck him on the floor. Honestly, I'm not even sure I can make it inside. The grass on the front lawn might have to do. I don't know who this version of me is, but I feel wild and reckless and gorgeous, and I never want it to end.

Ryder pulls into his driveway and hops out of the driver's seat, coming around to the passenger side and opening my door. I *just* have enough time to get my seatbelt off before he's pulling me out, wrapping his arms around my waist and covering my mouth with his. My entire body relaxes into him. God, I want him. I want him all over me. I want him everywhere he can possibly—

He breaks off the kiss, then plants another one on my cheek. "I'll be back."

I swear, I actually hear a record scratch. "What? We're not going to—"

"Time's up for tonight." He runs his fingers down my jaw, down my neck, and traces a path over my shoulder.

"*Shit*." Here I am, nipples hard against my bra, panties practically off already, and he has to go. "I mean—"

"Don't worry, Valentine," he says, giving me a squeeze that's not enough, that's just not enough. "There'll be time later for our too-spicy fling." He heads back around the car, his grin melting through my core.

"That's not sexy," I call after him.

"Yes, it is," he calls back, shutting the door. "And so are you."

Then he drives away, leaving me frustrated and squirming in his own front yard.

* * *

There are no streetlights on this road, not here by the lake, so it's almost total darkness once I turn off the lights in the cottage and lay down in my bed.

113

In my empty bed, without Ryder, a fact that seems almost too cruel. My body has been buzzing with him since the moment he dropped me off in his driveway across the street. I walked home feeling my own juices between my legs, and even now my nipples are still hard against the oversized t-shirt I threw on after the coldest shower imaginable.

It hasn't done anything.

A fling.

We agreed to a fling, and now all bets are off. This is exactly what Sharon meant when she said I should get out of the rut I was in about Conrad, right? It is *slightly* unfair to call it a rut, considering I've barely been in town three weeks, but...

...but who cares about Conrad when Ryder is so close, right now, that I could be at his front door in thirty seconds?

The fuck with the rules. He said it himself on the way back here, and it's pretty clear that a fling is going to mean something explosively hot. All I *really* have to do is pull the trigger.

I don't have his number.

I sit up in bed. I might have come back to Lakewood feeling like a small, diminished version of myself, but that doesn't mean I have to keep acting like that forever. And what's the risk? That I look stupid in front of Ryder? That's already happened more than once.

Plus, I have the perfect excuse to knock on his door.

I'm not waiting for the next time I bump into him for this to go on.

It's now or never.

I throw my legs over the side of the bed, grab my phone from the bedside table, and head for the door. I'm absolutely right. It's not thirty seconds before I'm standing in front of the Culvers' cottage.

It looks dark.

A shiver runs down my spine. This burst of courage was clearly a mistake. I should have at least put on regular clothes. I thought this would be sexy, but it's past midnight. There's no way that Ryder is—

"Valentine."

His voice, coming from the open front window, startles me so badly I let out a shriek that I have to stop with my hands. "Jesus, Ryder! What are you *doing*?"

He laughs out loud, his face coming into view in a sliver of moonlight. "What are *you* doing? You're standing outside my house in what looks like your pajamas in the middle of the night."

My cheeks burn. "I wanted to ask you something."

"Was it something that could wait until morning?"

I'm realizing now that if anyone drives by at this moment, they're going to see me standing in Ryder's yard without any pants on. At least I stopped for flip-flops.

"Not really."

"No?" Ryder's voice rises a little. "What's so pressing, then?" His voice curls into my gut. I'm wet just at the sound of him.

Now or never. "I wanted to keep our fling going. And I didn't have your number. Could I—" I hold up my phone like maybe I'm not being totally clear. "Could I get your number?"

He grins, his teeth flashing in the dark. "I'll give you more than that."

Chapter Twenty

RYDER

VALENTINE STANDING IN THE MOONLIGHT IN A T-SHIRT THAT just *barely* covers her ass, no pants, and her hair falling around her shoulders, catching the light, is the most beautiful sight I've ever seen.

My cock strains against my shorts.

I've been sitting here for an hour. Minnie had a rough time falling asleep, and the silence is almost too fucking precious to waste on sleep. I never thought I'd see Valentine making her way across her yard, then mine, with her head held high and shoulders back.

She hesitated at the front door, though, and I couldn't help myself. Her nipples went hard when I scared her, and they're still hard. She's not wearing a bra beneath the t-shirt.

A part of me wants to stay in the house. I shouldn't touch her. I shouldn't go any further than we've already gone, because if I do that—if I do anything more—I'm not going to be able to stop myself. A hot, fast, reckless fling sounds like heaven, but if I get in too deep, it's going to be hell. And I can't take any more of that right now.

But I also can't leave her out there. My hands ache to touch her.

"More than that?" She bites her lip, then grins. "Should I come in?" She shifts her weight toward the door.

"No."

Valentine stops dead at the word, eyes wide.

"No?"

"Stay right where you are." I see the shiver that runs through her. "Don't move."

"Okay," she says softly, but by the time the word is out of her mouth, I'm moving to the front door.

The air is humid and sultry as fuck, running over my skin the moment I step outside. Lakewood is quiet in a way that New York City never will be. It's so quiet that sometimes it hurts my ears. But tonight, for the first time, I notice the whisper of the wind through the trees. Over that, I can hear Valentine breathing. Her hard nipples press against her shirt with every single breath. She's trembling, even though the air is warm, her hand tight around her phone.

I'm almost to her when she crosses her arms over her chest and cocks her head to the side. "Ryder, what kind of game—"

I close the gap between us and wrap my arm around her waist, pulling her to me, pressing the length of her body against mine. I'm a little rougher than I intended, but Valentine gasps, and I look down into her eyes, colorless in the light of the moon, for any hint that she's not into this.

There is no such hint. Her entire body is leaning into me, and her free hand is on my bicep, her grip hard.

"Not a *game*," I say firmly. "A fling." I reach up to the wide collar of her shirt and yank it to the side, lowering my head to her collarbone. She gasps when I flick my tongue over the smooth skin there. The low almost-moans begin when I work my way up her neck, punctuating the kisses with words that have her pressing against me, somehow even closer than before. "A too-spicy fling. You're going to be on fire for me, Valentine."

She tilts her head back, giving me easier access to the side of her neck, and groans. "Shouldn't we take this inside?"

"And burn down my rental house? I don't think so." She feels so damn good in my hands, even when she makes a little show of pulling away.

"We're in the front yard..." Her voice is low and sexy near my ear.

I tighten my grip around her waist, and she doesn't resist a second time. "Haven't you ever had an orgasm in your front yard?"

Valentine sucks in a breath, and I kiss her neck slowly, moving upward one inch at a time until I reach her jawline. Her little gasps come quicker when I wrap one hand around the base of her jaw, holding her in place. A shiver that looks a hell of a lot like pleasure runs through her at my touch.

She hasn't seen anything yet.

"You can go if you want to," I murmur into her ear. "If you're worried about someone seeing—"

"I am." She's practically breathless, and it strikes me that she's telling me the absolute truth in this moment. There's no pretense, no bullshit, no hesitation—not real hesitation, anyway, not in this moonlight, which is so bright you could mistake it for a streetlight if you were half drunk.

I'm stone cold sober unless you count how intoxicated I feel being this close to Valentine. The urge to lower her to the ground and take her right the fuck now is so strong that every muscle aches with it. The only thing stopping me is the possibility that this hotter-than-hellfire fling might burn out too quickly if I make that move tonight. *No* part of me wants to risk that. I want this to last every moment that it can.

Valentine might be worried, but she's not so worried that she's willing to walk away from me. There's a spark in her eyes, just barely visible. I lean down and kiss her, deeper and harder, her tongue dueling with mine the moment I press past her lips. Jesus, she tastes good. She raises her hands to hold onto my arm like a drowning woman would hold a life preserver. I can feel her legs shaking.

I take that as a challenge.

I can make them shake harder.

I've got one hand on the back of her head, pulling her in, and she moans into my mouth, pressing herself against me, hard nipples brushing my chest through both of our shirts. That's all I need to lower my hand, grazing her waist, her hips, the front of her shirt, and the hem, low, low down.

When I hook a finger into the waistband of her panties, she makes a kind of animal noise that has my cock standing out so hard it hurts.

"Let me in," I growl into her ear, feeling that first bit of control snap into pieces and fall to the ground. I'm yanking her panties down, and her mouth is back on mine. "Let me *in*."

Valentine whimpers just a little as she spreads her legs, feet planted firmly on the ground, and finally, *finally,* I've got my fingers diving into her wet folds. She makes a sound like I've never heard any woman make before, and it turns electric and deep when I press my thumb against her clit.

I'm stroking her, playing her like a fucking violin, and Valentine loves it. Her hips rock against my hand, back and forth, back and forth, and she's getting slicker by the second. The kiss slips into moans against my mouth, and after a minute I realize she's saying something. I pull back.

"Please," she begs, and I feel like I've been struck by lightning. "Please make me come."

"Right here in the front yard?" I'm not teasing her anymore. I can tell how much this turns her on. "Right here, where anyone can see?"

"*Yes.*"

"You love being dirty like this, don't you?"

She opens her eyes wide, her hands sliding up to brace against my shoulders. She's trembling so hard now that I have to lower my hand to her back, hold her in place. I don't stop running my fingers over her hot slit for a second. We can talk all she wants. I'm going to keep up this rhythm until she explodes.

"Yes." The word is a whisper that goes straight to the center of me.

I turn her head to the side so I can growl into her ear. "You're not an innocent little waitress after all."

"I'm not," she says, and her breath hitches. "I'm so scared someone might see us—"

"You love the thought of being seen like this, with your legs spread wide for me, with my hand stroking that sweet pussy. You love it." Valentine tenses. She's right on the edge. "Say it for me, love. Say it."

"*I love it,*" she cries the words into the night air, and I take the opportunity to thrust two fingers into her opening, my thumb circling her clit.

I feel Valentine start to come, her muscles clenching around my fingers, and I brace for the wave to hit.

Chapter Twenty-One

VALENTINE

I've never come so hard in someone's front yard in my entire life.

I expect to be ashamed of it, but there's no room for shame when the orgasm hits, rocking me back and forth over Ryder's fingers. In the middle of the front lawn, my legs spread to let him in, clawing at his shoulders. It's a damn good thing he has one arm wrapped around my waist because the heat that rockets through me is so intense that I go weak in the knees.

"Oh, *fuck*," I breathe the words into his neck through clenched teeth. Is it wrong if I'm hoping, just a little, that someone drives by right now? That the headlights hit us both and the driver sees?

I never felt this way with Conrad. Conrad was the kind of guy who always wanted the doors closed and locked up tight behind us. He grew up wealthy—his dad's marketing firm, the one I got a job at—is a successful, traditional place that came out of seed money from his even wealthier grandfather—and when we did have sex, it was traditional, and always private. There wasn't any risk.

There *was* risk, of course, but we didn't know it until later.

That doesn't matter. I never wanted more of Conrad. I want more of Ryder, and I want it right now. My teeth chatter I came so damn hard, and his fingers are still pressing into me. Only I'm not done yet. It's been a long few weeks since I came back to Lakewood, and it's been longer since anything like this happened to me.

"I want...I want..." I want to be able to get a full sentence out, but it's impossible. Sheer electricity arcs through every inch of me and every breath I take is full of Ryder.

He grins, and my insides go molten hot. "I know what you want."

Then he hooks his fingers inside of me, finding a spot I never believed existed, and I explode again. This time, he really does have to catch me. I'm drowning in pleasure, and we haven't even had sex yet.

Holy shit. Holy *shit.*

When it subsides, I'm breathing hard, like I just ran several miles, and Ryder is looking down at me. He keeps his eyes on my face while he pulls his fingers out of my pussy, stroking all of my folds on the way out. I don't move. I don't even *think* about closing my legs. His touch is somewhere between gentle and firm and I'm even wetter, suddenly, than I was before.

I look back into his eyes. For once, I don't feel like I have to hide my face. Conrad was not an inspired lover, but I thought it was just me—I thought it would always be hard to have an orgasm. I thought I'd always have to put a hand over my eyes.

But I keep them firmly on Ryder's shoulders. An expression flickers over his face, something dark and sexy. "Don't look away from me," he says, his voice low.

"I wasn't going to," I whisper back. I wasn't going to, but now that he's said it, I feel white-hot need building up between my legs.

"Stay still." It's such a simple phrase, but all of my muscles tense with the effort. Ryder's eyes are catching the moonlight and reflecting it back at me. He strokes between my legs with three fingers. "Damn."

"Damn what?" My legs are starting to shake again. It's hard to get the words out, getting harder still to keep my eyes on his, but I can do it, I want to do it...

"You like that, don't you?" Another stroke.

"What?" Now my difficulty is that I want to throw my head back, want to let another orgasm grow and grow until it's a million points on the Richter scale, until all of Lakewood knows that

I'm out of my so-called rut and that I climbed out of it with Ryder Harrison, the sexiest person ever to step foot in this town.

But I'm not supposed to look away from him. He wants to see me come, see it on my face, and knowing that makes me even wetter. I've got juices running down the insides of my thighs, my panties pushed down around my knees...and a burning question pops up in my head.

Ryder's fingers are still working their magic in slow motion, and I'm clearly not thinking straight because I actually say the words out loud. "Were you...in the Army?"

"I'm doing *this* to you—" He does *this* again and now I have to close my eyes because keeping them open through that much pleasure is like keeping them open while you're sneezing. "—and you're asking me about my resume?"

"It's just that—" He does *this* some more. "—you have a way of...issuing commands that..."

"Makes you wet as hell," he says, pressing into my clit with that thumb of his. I'm going to come for the third time. I'm going to explode, fireworks-style, and he's going to have to carry me back to my house because I'm about to be *done for.* "I noticed that about you."

"I'm not into bondage," I blurt out, my mouth taking on a life of its own, my brain totally consumed by the fiery pleasure making tidal waves that start at my clit and engulf me completely.

"I didn't get that vibe from you," Ryder says as if we're just having a regular conversation, if one *had* regular conversations in which you growled things like that into the other person's ear while making them come on your fingers.

"Good...because—" I suck in another breath because whatever *this* is, he's taken it up several notches and I'm just...almost... *there...*

I open my eyes at the same moment that a light flashes against the front of the Culvers' house. Then comes the voice, echoing across the yard like an avenging angel, if that avenging angel was eighty years old and friendly with my parents.

"You two all right?"

I don't even have to look. I know who it is. It's Harold Finneman, from two lots down. He and his wife converted their cottage to a year-round home when I was in elementary school, and my mom has taken over countless meals when they go through their yearly health crises. And that aged voice is like ice water down my back. My entire body freezes, and not in a sexy way. I lean my head into Ryder's shoulder.

Nope. Nope nope nope. This is not the scenario I was imagining. I was imagining a pair of headlights sweeping by, illuminating our graceful forms and then disappearing into the night. Not Mr. Finneman out with his dog.

"Absolutely," says Ryder, and there's a hint of a laugh in his voice. Of course he would laugh. He's not the one standing here with his panties around his knees. He slips his hand out from between my legs and wraps it around my waist. There is no *way* Mr. Finneman is going to believe that this was just a friendly hug. But maybe, since it's dark...

And a full moon...

But hopefully dark enough to—

"We're great," Ryder continues, and I realize Mr. Finneman must still be standing there.

"Valentine? Is that you?"

I take in a deep breath through my nose and try not to melt into the earth.

This is my life.

I half-turn in Ryder's arms and give Mr. Finneman a big smile and a wave because I'm the kind of person now who smiles and waves in this kind of situation, I guess. "Hi, Mr. Finneman!" I call out. "Everything's fine!"

He's standing near the road, his flashlight pointed down at the concrete, and I can just make out his wrinkled face. "All right, Valentine." Another long pause. "Come on, Walter." Walter is his Golden Retriever. Walter, at least, has no idea what's happening.

They start to make their way down the road, and then, mother of God, Mr. Finneman pauses. "Oh, Valentine?"

I bite my lip, hard, trying my best to keep the smile on my face. Can he even see me? I don't want to know. "Yes?"

"What time does the Short Stack open up tomorrow? I was thinking of taking Walter for breakfast. To sit outside, you know. You have that water bowl there, and—"

"Six o'clock!" I try not to scream the words at the old man. "Six o'clock on the dot. That's when we open."

"Thanks, Valentine," he says, and then finally, blessedly, trundles off down the road with Walter.

The moment I turn back to Ryder, he presses his mouth against mine, but there's no way we can take back this moment. Not now. He tries, but he's laughing into my mouth.

Then his phone chimes. His monitor—his daughter.

He pulls away, still laughing. "That's my cue."

"Forget all of this," I tell him, reaching down to yank up my panties and retrieve my phone from the ground. I don't know when it fell, and I don't care.

"Not a chance, Valentine," he says from the doorway. I turn to go, my face burning in the dark. "Oh—wait."

I wheel back around. "What?"

"When does the Short Stack open tomorrow?"

I raise one finger into the air at him and turn my back as haughtily as I can. He's still laughing when I get to the road.

And I didn't even get his number.

Chapter Twenty-Two

RYDER

I FALL ASLEEP WITH LAUGHTER STILL ON MY LIPS, WHICH IS A strange feeling. It's been a long time since I could be this lighthearted about anything. The last few years haven't exactly been a cakewalk—not that I was expecting one when I joined the Army—but nothing could have prepared me for the hell of what happened with Angie.

I want to laugh like this every day of my life.

But even as I think it, even as I'm starting to fall asleep, the dark descending over my eyes, part of me pulls back from it. I want that *now*. But Valentine isn't a sure bet. Angie sure as hell wasn't, even with Minnie in the picture.

She woke up from some nightmare, standing at the side of

her Pack 'n Play and howling—not that I was going to be able to recover after Old Man Winter showed up on the road.

I'll never tell Valentine that I saw him coming. Who could miss that damn flashlight? But I wasn't going to stop doing what *we* were doing a second earlier than I had to. I don't care, anyway. I'm not going to be here long.

I feel a pang at that thought.

I used to think the same way when I was in Afghanistan, everything covered in sand and dust, the heat inside the tents more oppressive than actual hell. *I won't be here long. I won't be here long.* That would be true no matter how things played out. If an IED on the side of the road blew me to pieces, it'd be true. If I went home, it'd be true. Back then, not much mattered.

Now there's Minnie, and I have to keep moving. I can't stagnate in Lakewood and let somebody drag me down into the depths of some fucked-up relationship again.

Not that it would be that way with Valentine. In fact, I'm sure it wouldn't.

I'm just not sure that I can take it again if it *does* go south.

"Stop," I say out loud, into the dark. Wallowing isn't going to make this any better. I need to just enjoy the fuck out of this while it still lasts.

I open my eyes and look around at the outlines of the room in the moonlight. I'm not in Afghanistan. I'm not trapped in the city with Angie. And I'm not trapped in the city waiting for Angie to return. That's not going to happen.

I'm in Lakewood, only feet away from the hottest woman I've ever looked at or touched in my entire life. A woman whose blush makes me want to run my thumb over her cheeks and kiss her until she's melted in my arms.

A woman who, frankly, I'd like to bend over this bed and fuck absolutely senseless. And when Valentine comes? Stop the fucking presses. I could watch that all day.

I would if I *had* all day. If *she* had all day.

My hands are still aching with the need to touch her, touch her again, have her curves under my palms, when I finally fall asleep, hard as a rock.

* * *

"So, who's your new girlfriend?" Jamie stands in front of his grill, carefully rotating a cast of brats and hot dogs, while Poppy chases Minnie around the backyard. He has a nice backyard. It reminds me of the house we grew up in in Michigan. My dad spent weeks and weeks tending to the grass back there, making sure my mom's flowerbeds were weed wacked. He died of a heart attack when I was living in New York City with Angie. We didn't go to the funeral.

One of the bigger regrets of my life.

I raise my beer to my lips and take a sip. Jamie's shoulders are tense like he's expecting me to start an argument with him at any moment. I've only seen him a few times since I joined the Army, and none of them were what you would call cordial. That was largely my fault. I can't blame him.

"She's not my girlfriend."

He shoots a glance across the expanse of the deck at me. I'm leaning against the railing, half watching Minnie run around on her chubby little legs, half watching Jamie to see what kind of mood he's in this afternoon. I was surprised as hell when his text came in earlier inviting me to a cookout—a *cookout*—but even with the undercurrent between us, I'm not one to turn down free food. And if Poppy doesn't mind taking Minnie off my hands for an hour, everybody wins.

Or everybody *should* be winning. I wish Valentine were here.

"Seemed like a pretty important date." I scan Jamie's face again and catch the flicker of a smile at the corner of his mouth. That asshole. He always wanted to know about the girls I dated in school, too. But I'm not *dating* Valentine. I just want her so much I can almost taste her juices on my tongue. I want her so much that I'm walking around Lakewood with a permanent erection just thinking about the way she spread her legs and let me have my way with her.

It's a hot summer fling. Really. That's *it*.

"It was important in that—" In that the night ultimately

ended with that fiery hot scene in my front yard. If Minnie hadn't woken up, I'd have taken her inside. Maybe I should have anyway. No, best to keep that separate. We'll be gone by the end of the summer. I have to keep reminding myself that. I want to tell Jamie how Valentine looked in that oversized t-shirt, how we got caught out by that old man, but something stops me. I try again. "It's nothing serious."

"You wanted to get laid, didn't you?"

I roll my eyes. "Who doesn't?"

He shrugs. "You really should leave Valentine alone if you don't want to date her, you know."

I stare at Jamie. "I never told you her name."

He rolls his eyes, in such an exaggerated fashion that he almost falls over. "You're a dumbass. Valentine Carr is practically from here. When she showed up again a few weeks ago, everyone was talking about it. And anyway, she's the only waitress at the Short Stack. Unless they hired someone else for the crowds at Summer Surf." I make a gagging sound, and Jamie laughs. "I didn't decide to call it that."

"Even by *participating,* you're guilty of making this place too fucking cutesy."

Jamie clamps a hot dog between his tongs and turns it over, methodically moving to the next. "You're good at that. You're really good at that."

"Good at what? I'm just drinking a beer."

"Changing the subject."

"So, do you have plans for the big Summer Surf?" Summer Surf is the dumbest name for a festival the city council here could have come up with, namely because Long Lake, the lake that Lakewood is pressed up next to like Valentine was pressed up against me last night, is too small for surfing. It's just a bunch of people paddling around on those stand-up boards and drinking heavily.

Which, to be fair, is probably a pretty good time. I'm just not ever going to be caught dead paddling around like some idiot who couldn't find the ocean.

"Valentine's a really nice girl," says Jamie, like we're still having this conversation. "You shouldn't screw around with her."

"How do you even *know* her?"

"I eat breakfast just like everyone else. And I've heard she's great." Jamie cuts a glance across the deck at me. "She's *your* girlfriend. You should know."

"She's not my girlfriend." The more I say it, the more it sounds like a lie. But Valentine and I aren't ever going to go there. I can't risk it, and neither can she. She wants out of Lakewood again as much as I do.

At least, I think she does.

"Okay. Sure," says Jamie, looking back down at the array of meat on the grill. "I believe you."

Chapter Twenty-Three

VALENTINE

THE SUMMER HEAT CRACKS OPEN LIKE A BIG, FERTILE EGG over Lakewood, and the place floods with tourists. Sharon, naturally, takes full advantage, which means I hardly have any time to feel mortified over what happened in Ryder's yard. She keeps the Short Stack open for extended hours, serving breakfast well into the dinner shift.

I'm running ragged trying to keep up, but at the end of the day my apron is fat with tips. I need every penny I can get if I'm going to make it out of here by spring.

I'm motivated as hell, but in the lulls between breakfast and lunch and lunch and dinner, I can half-heartedly begin to admit that it's not getting out of Lakewood that's making me hustle between every table.

It's the heat between my legs. The only way I can keep my mind off of it is to focus completely on taking orders, rushing them back to the kitchen, and getting those trays out as fast as I can. And that heat is *all* Ryder.

But this is really about getting out of Lakewood. Ryder is just a means to an end. He's just a way to have fun, to cleanse my palate, get all the vestiges of fucking Conrad out of my mouth and soul.

For three days in a row, I wake up from intense dreams about that night in his yard and where it could have gone if only Mr. Finneman hadn't shown up with Walter. All I can do is dive into my shifts at the Short Stack. I don't dare knock on Ryder's door before I go to work—if he so much as kissed me, I'd never make it to my shifts—and ever since that night, I've been so busy from open to close that I can't keep my eyes open when I get home.

Trust me, I've tried. Last night I fell asleep on the sofa in the front room wearing my sexiest shorts and a bra, two shirts in my hands.

The sun has taken on an afternoon glow on Wednesday, and I'm still at the Short Stack. Sharon left when the last customer did after an extended pleading look in my direction. Yeah, she owns the place, but she had other plans. That's how she put it when she asked me to stay and prep for tomorrow's breakfast service.

"Valentine," she'd said in a low, serious voice, her eyes locked on mine. "Do something for me."

I'd given her a knowing smile. "You're going to ask me to stay late."

"I am." She gave me a solemn nod. "But only this once. And it's only because I have other plans."

I waited.

"Other...important plans."

"You know, Sharon," I'd said, tapping my fingers against the notepad in my apron. "If you're going on a date, you should just say so."

"Oh? Like you told me you went to the Mexican place with that sexy piece of—"

"That was *so* not a date."

"It *so* was. The entire place saw your little lip-lock in there." She clicked her tongue. "You thought that wouldn't get back to me? In *Lakewood*?"

I bit my lip. I wanted to give Sharon some snappy retort, some other line about how you can have a man's tongue claiming your mouth and still not be dating him.

I had nothing.

Hot *damn,* I want him so badly. I want to lie in a sticky mess underneath his sheets—or my sheets, or any sheets, really, as long as his gorgeous body is underneath them with me. I want his number on my cell phone, so I can tell him this...and maybe, via *text*, it wouldn't turn into some awkward scene. I almost laugh out loud thinking of Mr. Finneman's face when he saw us, and cover it just in time.

"Fine," I admitted because I knew she wanted out, and a strange tension in my chest was making me wish we'd stop talking about it. "We went out. But it wasn't a date. It's not serious. It's just—"

"Deliciously hot?" Sharon's eyes shine. "Look, if I were you—" She looks me up and down. "I wouldn't take no for an answer with him." She waves a hand in the air. "So what if he's not the marrying kind?"

It was a stab through my heart when she said it, but for the life of me, I don't know why. Ryder isn't the kind of man I ever imagined marrying. Yes, his body is what I would describe as epic, but he has a daughter...and plans to get out of Lakewood.

And so do I.

This is about *fun*. Sex and tacos. Not marriage. Jesus, Sharon.

I'm still thinking about what she said as I stand near the front counter, rolling silverware into paper napkins. It's the last thing I have to do before I head out. Sharon's words roll around in my mind, but I can't dwell on them for long. Ryder's eyes glinting in the moonlight keep catching my attention. I should have given *him* some action in return.

Why haven't we crossed paths since then, anyway?

My heart beats faster, a cold fear prickling in my gut. What if he's done with me already? What if he's avoiding me because I'm not his kind of woman? What if he wants nothing to do with a temporary small-town waitress? That's probably why I don't have his cell phone number. Once he's out of town, it won't be long before he finds an excuse to drop me like a hot potato.

I should drop *him* before that happens.

But those abs...that face...that *voice*...

I close my eyes, wrapping the silverware by feel, and picture his hands on me, sliding down to my hips, grasping firmly, and then one hand slipping between my legs, pressing right on my clit—

Fuck, it felt so good. It felt so good, and I'm so beat, that I let myself fall headfirst into the memory. It's like I'm watching from outside myself as my head tips back, eyes still closed, and I lick my lips, a low little moan escaping from between them.

And it's like I'm watching from outside myself as someone appears in the window, a wicked grin on his face, catching me full-on fantasizing about him.

The knock on the doorframe brings me back to reality, heat barreling into my cheeks, into every part of me. It's like I summoned him just by thinking about him. And he *definitely* saw me.

I can't look away from his eyes, his knock-me-out blue eyes. Another memory crashes into me—*Don't look away from me*—and there he is, right outside the window. He came here for me.

Ryder knocks again, that half-smile making my entire chest warm. "Valentine! Are you going to let me in?"

"We're closed," I say lamely, gesturing to the sign on the door. I'm *not* supposed to let him in. I should just finish up the silverware, and then'

What the hell am I *thinking*?

"Make an exception," he says through the glass. "I have to... *talk* to you."

The way he says it just about makes me burst into flames.

Chapter Twenty-Four

RYDER

I wasn't planning to burst into a closed restaurant and absolutely *claim* the waitress when I walked up to the Short Stack, but when I saw Valentine through the window—head back, lips parted, like she was moaning, like she did the other night—the rest of my resolve crumbled like a day-old pancake.

I have to be near her again, have to touch her.

She's still bright red as she makes her way to the door of the Short Stack and unlocks it, pulling it quickly open.

"Hey. I—"

Valentine cuts me off, sticking her head out the door and looking both ways like we're characters in a spy movie. Then she grabs me by the front of my shirt and yanks me inside, slamming the door behind us and locking it again with a quick twist of her wrist.

"You weren't followed, were you?" she says it like a joke, but I know she's half-serious.

"Not that I know of."

"Pay better attention next time you try to get me to break the rules."

I have to crack a smile at that. "Oh? Are we not supposed to be in here?" I step a little closer. There are only inches between us now, and I can smell her shampoo over the sweet scent of syrup that's settled into her clothes.

"No," says Valentine, crossing her arms over her chest. "We're definitely not. Sharon's rules."

"Then why'd you let me in?"

"You asked me to."

"I *told* you to." I step forward, lean down. "I told you to, and you liked it."

Valentine shivers, but I see her smile out of the corner of my eye. "So what if I did?"

"I'm sorry." I'm so close that it would only take the tiniest movement to touch her, but I don't. My entire body hums with it, a bright feeling running down into my fingertips. I used to play this kind of game in Afghanistan. Hold back from doing the thing I want to do—jerk off, eat an MRE, pick up a beat-up book—until the energy is practically pulsing out of me in waves.

"For what?"

"For interrupting you."

She blushes a deeper shade of pink, then shakes her head. "You saw that?"

"I saw you thinking about something that turned you on."

Valentine turns her face away from me and bites her lip. "Well, maybe I was, and maybe I—"

That's it. It's like a lightning strike to my core. I can't wait any longer. I can't do this any longer. I've been beaten at my own game because I'm at my limit when it comes to the teasing. It doesn't seem possible—it's only been a few days since we started this *fling*—but I need her now.

She gasps when I take her in my arms, one arm around her waist, the other hand turning her face toward mine. The movement has just a hint of roughness in it, but in Valentine's eyes, I see nothing but liquid heat. She fucking loves this.

"I *saw* you," I repeat. "You were thinking about us, weren't you?"

"Yes," she whispers, then clears her throat. "I've been thinking about you for days. It's stupid because one date shouldn't—"

I silence her by covering her mouth with mine and she leans into the kiss, our tongues dancing. Fuck me, I've never kissed anyone like Valentine. I've never wanted to kiss anyone more.

Then I start backing her up, into the kitchen. "I've been thinking about us, too. All day, every day. I can't stop, Valentine. *I want you*." I growl the last three words into her ear, and the air in the room shifts, turns sultry and serious.

Valentine's back connects with a prep table and she sucks in her breath, grasping for the edge. "Ryder, I—"

I bend down and do what I've wanted to do since she left my front yard the other night. I press my lips against the creamy skin of her neck, just above the collar of her shirt, and work my way up toward her earlobe, flicking it with my tongue when I get there.

"Ryder—"

"That's right," I say into her ear. "Say my name. I'm going to make you moan it, scream it—"

"You can't—"

"I can, and I will."

Valentine is trembling in my hands, but her eyes are wide, bright with anticipation. "Sharon could walk back in at any moment."

"Let her."

"But I might—"

"Get to come so hard you forget all about Sharon and everyone else?" I lift her onto the table, my hands on the perfect curves of her ass. Valentine's arms automatically go around my neck.

Her face is the fucking picture of desire, green eyes half-closed, lips half-open, and I take that as a resounding yes.

The little black shorts she wears for her waitressing shifts come off in my hands, slipping down over her knees with a yank, dropping to the floor.

"Here's the thing, Valentine," I say, spreading her knees apart with my hands and stepping between them. "We agreed that there was only one rule."

"Right," she says, breathless. "It's just a fling."

"So why..." My hands seek out the waistband of her panties. They're pink and stretchy, some kind of performance fabric. "Do we keep..." I take them in my fists. "Dancing around this like we don't want to fuck?" One yank and the panties tear away from her in my hands. I drop the remains to the floor alongside her shorts, and then I bend my head between her legs, spread her open a little wider, and lick the entire length of her pussy.

Her unbelievable, gorgeous pussy. She's waxed it bare, and the smoothness of her skin just about pushes me over the edge.

"Oh, *fuck.*" Valentine braces her arms against the table and tilts her head back, just like she was doing before, only now she has a good reason. I lick her sweet slit, once, twice, three times, tasting her juices, and then I'm going for my own belt.

When I stand up, Valentine reaches for me, her hands firm on my shoulders. For a split second, I think she's trying to stop me, and a tiny part of me dies inside, but then she looks me straight in the eye. "Are we being honest?"

It's a strange question, but in this moment I don't have time to think about what the fuck she means. I take it at face value. "Yes."

"Then I should say..." She sucks in another breath. "I want you to fuck me. Right here, on this table, right now." Then she blows out that breath between rounded lips. "*Please*, Ryder. Please fuck me. I need it."

Chapter Twenty-Five

VALENTINE

I DON'T KNOW WHO I'VE BECOME—A WOMAN WHO BEGS FOR SEX in the kitchen of the cafe she works in, apparently—but I can't stop the words from coming out of my mouth. My entire body is on fire for the man between my legs, but he's not close *enough*. I want it to be even hotter. I don't care if it's so spicy it burns my mouth. I have to have him. Anyway, I'm not exactly begging, I'm just confirming that I want this, and I want it badly.

Ryder's shorts hit the floor with a soft *thud*, and I look down to the most perfect cock I've ever seen.

He's *hung*, and it's flawless. No strange curves, just smooth skin. I don't have to touch him to know that it must be painfully hard.

I don't have to touch him, but I do. I reach down and grip the length of him. His cock pulses in my hand. A low growl escapes Ryder's mouth.

I'm not the only one who's going crazy waiting for this.

All at once his hands are cupping my face, callused against my skin, and he's tipping my face up toward his. I think it's going to be another rough kiss, our mouths colliding like they did in the dark of his front yard, but instead, he kisses me so gently that tears come to my eyes.

The moment kaleidoscopes out. My hand is still wrapped around him, but he's kissing me like I'm a precious, fragile object, like we've been together for years, like we're alone in our bedroom, the door locked behind us, and not about to screw like animals on a prep table in the Short Stack's kitchen. It sends heat spiraling down between my legs. I'm wet for him. I'm wet for *this*. But there's a strange ache in my chest. I want more than this. I want more, but there's no way I can tell him.

Then he pulls back and looks into my eyes, a breath caught in his throat. I can't read his expression, and for a long moment, we're frozen.

I can't take it. What is this, even? It doesn't feel like a hot summer fling. It doesn't feel like something you can just discard at the end of August like an old bathing suit.

It's up to me to end it.

"Fuck me," I whisper, the words harsh against the tenderness of his kiss.

Okay. *Now* I'm begging.

It snaps him out of whatever that fantasy was, and it could be anything—the two of us in a house with a white picket fence, some vacation in Las Vegas, I have no idea—but his eyes narrow and that sexy grin reappears. "I won't make you ask twice," he says, and then he comes back for more.

This time, he doesn't hold back.

And God, do I love it.

I let myself go under the force of his kiss, raw and powerful. I let go of his cock and hang on for dear life, the muscles of his arms flexing under my hands.

Then his hands are on my waist, on my hips, pulling me to the edge of the table. Then he's lining himself up, the thick head of his cock at my opening. I'm soaking wet, I've never been more ready in my life, I need him to take me, I need him to erase every last place that Conrad ever was and free me from this nagging feeling that I'll never get out of Lakewood again, *fuck me, fuck me.* I beg silently, biting my lip, tilting my hips toward him.

He enters me in one long thrust.

Ryder takes up every inch of space, claiming my body for his own, but it's such a delicious stretch that I can hardly stay on the table. I want to throw myself forward, tackling him to the ground, and ride him, but I know for a fact that Gerald would have a fit if he ever found out I'd been screwing a man on his pristinely mopped floor.

The table will be easier to clean. And we'll have to clean it because I'm pretty sure it's already *pretty* wet.

My nipples are hard. I wonder if Ryder can feel them through my bra, through the two shirts between us, because I can't let go. I'm wrapped around him tightly, and the sensation of being filled by him is so damn perfect that I don't want him to pull back for another thrust.

Only I *do.*

Ryder makes the decision for both of us, rocking back for another powerful thrust, his hands firm on my hips. He's so tightly muscular that I can hardly stand it. There's not an ounce of fat on him. He gets into a rhythm with a growl that he lets out through clenched teeth.

"You're too good for this."

The words don't make sense at first, and then they do. "No. I'm just bad enough." Even through the haze of pleasure wrapping itself around all of my senses, I'm pretty pleased with that line. For once in my life, something unbelievably fucking hot is happening, and I'm enjoying the hell out of it. It feels good to be just a little bit reckless, just a little bit out of control.

I open my mouth to tell Ryder to fuck me harder, fuck me faster, to give myself over to this with total abandon. "*Yes.*" It's one breathless word, and then I find my voice. "Harder. *Please*, harder—"

A loud pounding on the door stops my heart mid-beat and turns the words into a shriek.

At the sound of someone's fist making contact with the metal storm door on the side of the Short Stack, I just *react.* So much for being sexy and reckless. Instead, I shove Ryder backward with all my strength and leap off the table. Only my panties are a shredded pile of cloth on the floor.

"My panties!" I cry, forgetting to keep my voice down. I don't want to put my shorts on without them because the shorts are tight, and I'm soaked. "How am I supposed to wear my shorts?" I sweep the shorts off the floor and thrust them at Ryder like he can help me.

He laughs and bends for his shorts.

Fine. I'll wear the damn shorts. It's an effort to pull them up, and the fabric sticks between my legs.

Very sexy.

"Hello?" The knock comes again, along with a muffled greeting from outside.

My mind goes into overdrive. How much did this guy hear? What is he going to do? Maybe he'll just leave.

But he doesn't leave. He knocks again as Ryder zips up his shorts and does his belt.

"I swear to God, Valentine, every time we—"

"*Shhh.*" I hiss at him, shooting him a look.

He laughs again. "Are you going to get that?"

I yank open the inner door, turning my back on Ryder in the process and drawing myself up to my full height. Out the corner of my eye, I see Ryder bend to reach for something on the floor and shove it into his pocket.

My panties.

Jesus.

"Hello?" The word comes out sharply, and I immediately regret it. The guy standing in the alley next to the restaurant can't be more than twenty. *You're at work, Valentine. Act like it.* I clear my throat and try again. "Hi. How can I help you?"

He's wearing a red shirt with a red baseball cap. All of it looks company issued. Oh, shit. The meat delivery.

I've just been interrupted mid-coitus by a truck full of meat.

"I'm from Pinehill Farms," the guy says, recovering. "I've got a shipment—"

"Great." I want this conversation to be over so I can go back to doing...Ryder. "You can bring the crates in and put them in the walk-in—"

"—of sausages," he finishes, and I hear Ryder try to stifle a laugh behind me. "I'm going to need you to double-check that the order is correct, though." He lifts a clipboard and looks down. "Extra-long sausage links," he says, without batting an eye. Then his face brightens. "Thick, too."

Chapter Twenty-Six

RYDER

I T'S MORE OF A PROCESS THAN YOU'D THINK, CONFIRMING THE girth and length of a shipment of sausages. This delivery kid is *thorough,* asking Valentine to look at every single one of the wrapped packages in the crates along with him. "Yes," she says, again and again. "This matches with the original order. I'm sure Gerald will be very pleased."

"The nice thing is," he says, "when the sausages are thick like this, they really fill out a breakfast plate. It's not some kind of—" He looks to the ceiling like he's searching for the right words. "There's not a big empty hole between the pancakes and the eggs. Know what I mean?"

Valentine stares at him, open-mouthed. "I mean," she says,

and the kid looks up from the crates, the expression on his face on the verge of being super worried that something is fucked up with these sausages. "You can't possibly…" her voice trails off, and I see it on her face, the moment she realizes that this delivery guy is *sincere* in his desire to make sure every one of these thick sausages is up to snuff. "You know what? These are great." Valentine's voice leaves no room for argument.

"Are you sure?" He gestures to the last two crates. "There are two more that we could—"

"No." She raises a hand, the universal sign to shut the fuck up and get out of the restaurant. I'm in total agreement. I want to be done with the sausages, hilarious as they are, and get back to the sexy spicy summer fling portion of the evening. "This delivery is absolutely perfect—" She squints her eyes, reading his nametag. "Nick. You are free to go."

"Okay," he says, hesitating. "But I just need to make sure that—"

"Nick." Valentine is breathing in a very *very* calculated manner now, like she might explode if Nick doesn't get the hell out of the Short Stack and leave us alone. "Everything is fine. You will not be in trouble if one of these sausages is…damaged, somehow." Even through her need to get him out of here, she can't quite contain her laughter when she says the word *sausages.* It's too much, really. "I will take full responsibility for all of the sausages."

Nick glances toward the door. He probably has somewhere to

be, a nice guy like Nick. Some sweet girlfriend who doesn't mind that he delivers truckloads of sausages for a living. He'll probably turn out to be an investment banker or some shit, later in life. He has that kind of face. No, I'm wrong. He's way too earnest to be an investment banker. But the sweet girlfriend? I'll be damned if I'm wrong about *that.*

"Okay," Nick says again, and this time he adjusts his cap, puts his clipboard down at his side, and moves toward the door at a fucking snail's pace.

Valentine can't stand it.

She steps in front of him, yanking the door open, and puts her hand on his shoulders.

"Whoa," says Nick, but Valentine doesn't let up. She guides him out the door. "Let me know if anything isn't satisfactory. You can contact me at—"

Valentine slams the door, leaving Nick reciting his email for nobody.

She turns back to me, eyes blazing with heat.

"I'm done with this shit," she says, and in one fluid motion strips her shirt over her head.

I can't help but let out a laugh. "Don't you think that this is a sign of—"

"I don't believe in *signs*," Valentine spits, and then she pounces.

She literally comes at me through the air, and it's only by the grace of the entire fucking universe that I manage to brace myself for her weight at the last second. Still, the force of it sends us toward the floor. On the way down, out of habit, I stick my hand out. The way we were standing, just next to the prep area, means that I catch a bag of flour with my fingertips.

A bag of flour. What the hell is *that* doing there?

I'm still considering it when the bag falls one second after we do, hitting the ground and exploding.

Flour flies up and out in every single direction like a bomb, and for a second my stomach twists at the sight of it. But I'm still focused on taking the impact of the floor away from Valentine. I'm so focused on it that it takes me a few extra moments to realize that we've already landed, that the flour flying through the air is the only thing that hasn't settled on the tile floors yet.

Valentine is in my arms, her mouth a perfect O, her hair white with flour. *Everything* is covered. I swallow the last of my panic, the last of the nightmare, and let the laughter take over.

Valentine isn't laughing. She presses her lips into a thin line and then pushes up into a sitting position, straddling my hips. Only she's fucking *covered* in flour. So am I. There's absolutely no way we're turning this into a sexy interlude anymore.

She tilts her head back, looking toward the sky, then raises two fists.

"No!" She cries, shaking them at the sky, the floor, the demolished bag of flour. "Damn it! I was *so close!*"

Valentine steps out of my shower, raising the towel to her hair and rubbing the excess water out of it. Then she examines the ends. "I think it's all out. *Ugh*."

I come over and assess the situation. "I think it's all out, too."

It's a quiet, peaceful moment, a haven in the midst of exploding bags of flour and sausage deliveries. The bathroom is hot and humid, but there was no way in hell I was going to let Valentine step out of that shower by herself.

We don't need any more slips and falls.

She wraps a second towel around her waist and looks up at me, her hair falling in a wet sheet over her shoulders. "Okay," she says finally. "I think I'm ready to move on."

My gut plummets to the floor. Move on from what? Our fling? It's barely started yet.

"I don't want to talk any more about what happened at the restaurant tonight," she continues, looking me straight in the eye. "I don't want to hear any more about how being *too into a person* can cause accidents."

I nod solemnly, a warmth blooming in my chest at her serious tone. "No more jokes."

"No more jokes," Valentine echoes. "I'm done with all the jokes. I'm done with running away." She straightens her back. "If we're going to have a fling so hot it can burn my mouth off, then I want to do that. *I want to actually do it*."

I move toward her, finding the edge of the towel, and unwrap it. It hits the floor with a muted whisper. "Right now?"

"Right now," says Valentine.

I scoop her up into my arms and head for the bedroom.

Chapter Twenty-Seven

VALENTINE

RYDER CLOSES THE DOOR BEHIND US, AND IN THE HUSH OF HIS bedroom, something shifts.

It's late. It took forever to clean up the flour in the kitchen, sweeping it all into one of the oversized trash bins in the back. By the time we were done, Ryder had to pick up his daughter, Minnie, at daycare.

I went with him.

Maybe it was stepping over some line, but I couldn't bring myself to let him out of my sight. The few moments we'd had on that table in the Short Stack had felt so good that my body is still humming with them, even though we were rudely interrupted by my damn *job*. It was too good of a moment to let slip through my fingers, so I went to pick up Minnie at Norma's.

Norma's face lit up when she answered the door. "Valentine!" she'd said, and my heart sank. Norma's been in the childcare circuit so long that she was my after-school babysitter growing up. "How are you, Norma?"

Her eyes had gone from me to Ryder, a wide smile spreading over her face. "Wonderful. Just wonderful." She'd opened her mouth to say more, but Minnie had run up behind her then, jumping up and down at the sight of her dad.

It warmed my heart. It really did. And then it broke, just a little, because something about that little voice made me want to stay in Lakewood.

I dismissed the thought, though. It wasn't the time to think of Lakewood. It was time to get Minnie home for a final snack and then into her bedroom.

Once she was asleep, Ryder led me into the bathroom by the hand and helped me strip off all my clothes. Slowly. Thoughtfully. Like he wanted to savor the moment.

Then we'd spent a romantic hour getting all that godforsaken flour out of our hair.

But now we're clean, the mistakes of the day washed away, and something about the quiet in the room makes me feel...

At home.

I take it all in: the queen-sized bed with a plain blue comforter. The low dresser. That's it. That's all the furniture there is. It's obvious that Ryder spends no time decorating.

It's also obvious that I don't care.

I turn back to him, to where he's standing by the doorway, watching me look at his stuff. The only thing worth looking at in this entire room is his unbelievable body. Ripped abs, every muscle toned to perfection. I want him, and I don't want a single interruption. How about that, universe? Not a single interruption.

The moment is stretched so tight that I can hardly stand it. My heart is about to beat out of my chest. I'm surprised it hasn't flown right out of my ribs. Because even though we've been in his shower, naked, the sight of a shorts-clad Ryder makes it feel like there's no air in the room. Or maybe too much air. Hard to tell.

I tighten my grip on the towel I have around me, suddenly feeling a little bit shy. I don't know why. He's seen everything there is to see, and then some. He's seen me running the hell away from him, back into my own front yard. He's seen me with a mouthful of hot sauce at the Mexican restaurant. What could possibly embarrass me now?

None of that matters. Not in this moment. It doesn't even matter that we started fucking back at the Short Stack. This is a thousand times more intimate. I'm standing right in his personal space, and I don't want to leave.

"Is that—" The words stick in my throat, and I have to clear it. "Is that locked?"

He gives me a grin that makes all of me go hot and melty. I can feel myself getting wet. If I had panties on, they'd be soaked.

The *last* thing I want right now is to have panties on.

"Yes, Sweet Valentine," he says, "it's locked."

He started calling me Sweet Valentine on the way to his place. Apparently, giving the sausage delivery guy the time of day is enough to make a person sweet. When he said it in the car the first time, I snorted.

But now, standing here in the lamplight, it has a different ring to it.

"Nobody's going to interrupt us?" I ask the question even though there's no way he can guarantee anything. He can't even know the answer.

"You and I both know," he says, his hands going to my waist, "that I can't promise you that."

His lips on the side of my neck, running down in a trail of heat, make me forget what I was worried about. "I don't—" I suck in a breath when he works his way down to my collarbone. "I don't know what I was saying."

"You don't have to say anything." Ryder puts one hand on mine and gently loosens my grip on the towel until it falls to the floor. He bites his lip, looking down at me.

"Do you like what you see?" I don't know why I'm asking, only that there's a strange ache in my chest. It's been a long time since anyone looked at me like this.

His answer is to take my hand and put it on the front of his shorts.

He's hard as a rock.

"You should take those off," I whisper, and he does. I've never seen a man drop a pair of shorts so quickly, but then there he is, in all his glory.

And fuck, he is *glorious.*

My throat goes tight, like I'm going to cry, which isn't the kind of reaction I expected from myself. This isn't supposed to be some emotional lovemaking. It's just a summer fling. It's *just* a summer fling, while we're both here. Time's limited.

I give my head the tiniest shake, banishing the thoughts. Those thoughts can go to hell. It's not worth considering, anyway. Ryder might not be the kind of man who will turn around and betray the fuck out of me like Conrad was...but then again, I haven't known him long enough to be sure of that. I knew Conrad for seven years before he turned on me. I've known Ryder—well, not long enough.

"Who needs it?" I whisper as Ryder steps closer, and he pulls back. No, no, *no*. I don't want him to pull back.

"What?"

"Nothing. Nothing at all. Trust me."

Then he's kissing me, his lips moving powerfully against

mine, and I don't care about any of that shit anymore. I might as well be back at the Short Stack, spread open for him on the prep table—I'm that hot, that *ready*.

When he lifts me in his arms and moves us to the bed, it's all over.

Chapter Twenty-Eight

RYDER

I take my sweet time with Valentine because I can't force myself to rush this.

I can't force myself to fuck her like I'd fuck any of the other nameless, faceless women I've been with in moments of desperation. Angie consumed most of my time once I got back from Afghanistan, but before that, it was just a series of one-night stands.

I've got nothing against the hot fuck. I could have spent hours with her in the Short Stack. But something about the way she looks right now, her hair still damp from my shower, makes my chest ache.

I want to see Valentine like this every day. Every day in the fall, every day in the winter, every day in the spring. One summer with her isn't enough.

My head swims with how fucking perfect she is, how her skin is so creamy and smooth, how her curves are so delicious that I want to lick every inch of her.

Instead, I settle for spots that I hope will drive her wild.

I start at her collarbone, swirling my tongue along those ridges there, and get a low sound of appreciation from her throat. Then I work my way down. When my tongue meets her nipples, the moan gets a little louder, a little more *involved.*

"I like the sound of that," I murmur into her ear. Valentine curls against me, her body pressing against mine in a way that makes my chest feel strange and tight, before spreading herself out again on the comforter.

"I like the sound of you," she says.

"Are you flirting with me?"

"No," she says, opening her eyes to grin at me. "I don't have to do that. We have an agreement."

It's true—it's fucking true that we agreed on the length of this little fling—but hearing about it right now sends a bolt of pain through my heart. It takes me by surprise. Valentine is instantly worried.

"What did I say?"

No. I am *not* going to let the truth derail the pleasure I've been waiting to give her since... since the moment I saw her, at least. If I'm being honest.

I give her my biggest, most roguish grin, and her face immediately echoes it back. "I just remembered something boring I have to do later."

"What's that?"

"Not fuck you."

She throws her arms around my neck then, pulling me down to her and kissing me fiercely. It's like fireworks, a thousand sparklers running through my nerves, and we move effortlessly into another mode. The too-hot mode. The fuck-me-now mode. And I fucking love it.

I love her.

The thought comes to me without warning, and it's so stupid that I almost laugh out loud. If I weren't consumed with spreading Valentine's legs, running my hands down her thighs, teasing her with my fingertips hovering just outside her most sensitive space, I'd do it. Love her? No.

But I could. I could love this woman, this sweet, awkward, spitfire of a woman who was only afraid of me for a split second when we met. Who doesn't see me as a dad drowning in the weight of the fucked-up past. I *could* love her.

Shit. I could *love* her.

Then the part of my brain that's interested in dwelling on

some are-we-or-aren't-we bullshit shuts down, and I'm lost in her.

* * *

I make her come with just my fingers, even as she tries to put me first. Do I *want* to let her get on her knees at the foot of the bed and take me into her mouth? Yes. Hell yes. But for once in my life, I'm more interested in making sure she is satisfied beyond belief.

For once this summer, there's nobody bursting through the door, no random foods to catch her off guard, and no *sausage deliveries,* for God's sake.

I learn that Valentine likes to have her clit rubbed in a very specific way, and she likes to have it done often. The first time I make the circles with my fingertips the perfect size her whole body tenses, and then relaxes, and she sucks in a huge breath.

"This," I whisper in her ear, making those circles in just the right rhythm. She's almost straddling me, her face pressed close to mine, her legs held apart by my hips. Valentine trembles against me, gritting her teeth.

"What?"

"This is what's so hot it'll burn your mouth."

"My mouth—" she can hardly string the words together. "Is fine." Then another moan escapes her on the tail end of a breath.

"You're so close."

"I'm *so* close," she breathes into my ear. There are a million stars bursting in my chest. I don't know if I've ever felt so right in my life, here in the lamplight with Valentine, on my bed, behind not one but two locked doors.

Now I just need to make her come.

She's right on the edge, and she buries her face into my shoulder like it's too much to let it show.

Oh, no. I'm not having that.

"Look at me," I whisper, and she pushes up so that our eyes meet, her red hair tousled. She bites her lip.

"This seems... like a recipe... for disaster."

"It seems like a recipe for an orgasm. Speaking of..."

She shoots me a glare that makes me laugh, makes my cock pulse between us. "Don't fool around, Ryder."

"Fool around? I'd never."

I tease the head of my cock against her opening, my hand working between us. I can see her starting to blink, starting to get overtaken by the wave of pleasure, but she's fighting hard to maintain eye contact. It's brave as hell. I thought it was cute, all the shit that kept happening, lighthearted as fuck, but for Valentine, those things must have been mortifying. Yet here she is, showing me all of her without flinching at all.

Her mouth opens just slightly as I push into her entrance, still teasing her. Spots of color come to her already-pink cheeks. "Ryder..." The word is half warning, half plea.

I work another inch into her tight, wet opening, and she

rocks her hips back against me. I won't give her anymore. Not until...

I pick up the pace with my fingers, just a bit, *just* a bit, and Valentine's entire body reacts, her hands clenching on my chest.

"*Oh...*" she breathes, and then she's over the edge, hips moving out of control, slamming back. At the peak of her orgasm, I thrust into her, all the way, taking up every inch.

I almost explode inside her right then and there. That's how good it feels. Oh, my God, so fucking good.

It wouldn't matter if the entire fire department burst in right now. I wouldn't even miss a beat.

Valentine starts rocking with a new rhythm, and I let it take me away.

I might never come back.

Chapter Twenty-Nine

VALENTINE

NOTHING AGAINST THE PREP TABLE AT THE SHORT STACK, but I would take Ryder's bed *anytime*.

No matter what happens, I think I'll always have a certain fondness for this dark blue comforter, the mattress with a little give, and the pillows that smell like him. How could I not? The things he's doing to me are a damn revelation.

He's hard as steel, so hard that when I reach down and take him into my hand, there's almost no give. I don't know how he can possibly wait...

But he does.

He spreads me out on the bed and strokes me until I'm trembling with a kind of slow-burn pleasure that I've never felt before.

Not with Conrad. Certainly not with any of my fumbling high school boyfriends. They never had the patience or the skill.

When he tumbles into bed with me, I'm already so far gone, so adrift in a delicious pleasure that's not as scorching as the hot sauce at the Mexican restaurant. It doesn't take me by storm. It inches up and outward from my clit, where he's focusing most of his attention and takes me over like the little waves on the lake that turn into big, rolling movements in the water.

I come for the first time on top of him, every inch of his perfect muscles on display, rocking against mine. I never liked being on top. Not until now.

And when he tells me to look at him while I come, everything that's happened before flies right out of my head. I forget how stupid I must have looked shooting whipped cream right into his face. I forget how awkward it was that he felt the need to *kiss me to save me* at the Mexican place. I forget all of it. Nothing matters except looking into his blue eyes.

In those eyes, there's nothing but a deep care. With a shock, I realize that it's all for me.

This moment between us has erased the darkness from Ryder's eyes, erased the sensation that he's waiting for something terrible to happen. Right now, I know with all of my heart that nothing is going to ruin this.

What a fucking *tease* he is. I'm so deep into the pleasure that he's giving me with two fingers—two fingers that have more skill than all of Conrad's body—that it almost pushes me right over the edge when he enters me, just a little.

I want more. I have to have more.

And when he thrusts in, all of him at once, in the middle of the first wave of my orgasm—well, holy *shit*. I've never felt anything so good in my entire life.

Ryder starts a rhythm that feels like it was meant to be. His hands on my hips are strong and confident, adding to their dance, and I never want him to let go. Never. Never. *Never*.

I lose track of the sounds coming out of my mouth. I lose track of everything but his blue eyes, but his thickness taking up every inch of available space. I come again, a shorter peak than the first time but just as intense, and this time I have to close my eyes.

Ryder starts to lose it when I push up on his chest, sitting back so I can breathe. I'm about to pass out from how all encompassing this feels, and I have to breathe. But sitting up only changes the angle of his cock, hitting all-new spaces inside of me.

"Oh, my *God*," I breathe, and then he snakes his hand back between my legs and presses the pad of his thumb to my clit.

It's a shattering orgasm, making me throw my head back, and when I open my eyes again, he's grinning at me, wickedly, the pillows behind him framing his face.

"There's nothing I'd rather do than watch you come on my cock," he says into the relative quiet of the room.

"Oh yeah?" I can hardly catch my damn breath. "Well, if that's true, then—"

He does something with his hips that deepens the thrust, making me react, rocking my hips against his, and that thumb again—

I'm not going to be able to do this much longer. I don't even know if my body can *handle* this much pleasure. It never reached this level with anyone else, and it rages through me, wave after wave, shoulders to fingertips, waist to toes. *This* is like a glass of water in the desert. It might be too much, but I also don't know how I've lived this long without it.

As I'm coming down, Ryder is picking up the pace, but I can't stay upright any longer. He seems to sense it because he rolls us both over so that he's on top, propped up on his elbows, grinning down at me, thrusting in and out, in and out. I wrap my legs around him.

I've never felt sexier in my life. I've never felt more wanted, more secure, in my life.

I can't let this summer go.

I know that I can't.

It sends a pain like breaking glass through my heart and he sees it on my face, but he doesn't miss a beat. He brings his hand to my cheek, brings his lips to my jaw, pressing there. "No, Sweet Valentine, don't think about it."

"How do you know—" It's a choked whisper.

"Just be here with me. Just *be here with me*." And just like that, I'm pulled back into him, into the raw, manly scent of him, into the muscled body that's shielding me from the world, into the in and out of his cock, in and out, in and out, wave after wave, bringing me closer and closer to the top and then sending me careening over into another orgasm. Another and another. I can't tell when one ends and another begins.

I'm a liquid puddle of desire by the time he reaches for his bedside table. I hear the drawer open and close and the tear of a foil wrapper, and then he's out—oh, God, the emptiness—and entering me again a few moments later. I put my hands on his hips and let myself feel the movement from every available angle—the way he brings himself close to the edge—am I whispering naughty nothings in his ear or am I just hallucinating it?—and then I feel it in my hands when he loses control, our bodies colliding again and again.

At some point, I don't know when, everything goes still and dark.

Peace.

Chapter Thirty

RYDER

I COME SO HARD IT MAKES THE CORNERS OF MY VISION BLURRY, but things don't exactly end there. At least, I think they don't. Valentine is curled around me, trembling. She kisses the corner of my jaw, my earlobe, and across my cheek, hot and sweet, every print of her lips burning on my skin. I *think* she has one or two more little orgasms, her hips rocking against me before she falls asleep.

I haven't slept with anyone—*really* slept with anyone—like this for a long time.

Maybe ever.

Valentine curls against my side, her naked, perfect breasts

pressed up against my ribcage. She breathes in and out in a rhythm that reminds me of waves on the lakeshore. Her red hair is everywhere. I can see it all because neither of us thought to turn off the light.

Only I can't bring myself to move. Not a single muscle.

I want her to stay like this, with me, for as long as possible.

It only takes a few minutes for my arm to start to ache. Still, the weight of her body against mine feels...secure, somehow. Safe. A shelter in the storm.

It wasn't supposed to be like this. I wasn't supposed to need her. I'm not supposed to need anything from anyone in this town, or any other town. But her body against mine could become a little bit of an obsession.

Who am I kidding? It's already an obsession, even if I'm only willing to admit it in the privacy of this bedroom. It's not quite my bedroom, but it'll do. With Valentine next to me the room doesn't matter at all.

My eyelids are heavy. I never get enough sleep, not with Minnie around, and I'm pretty damn spent from what just happened here.

It's been a long road.

I raise my hand to my mouth to stifle the laugh that bursts through my chest. The thought of Valentine looking at all those sausages, so patient, while that poor kid stood there... He had to have known that we were hooking up. Had to. I mean, how could he not? I never felt an ounce of jealousy for him or his sausage-delivering life, which is rare these days.

Although I haven't been envying anyone else's life now that Valentine and I are playing this game.

It's not a game, though.

I can hardly keep my eyes open, drifting off in between thoughts. Is it really a game? No, I don't think it is. I think I want more from her, but I'm not going to ask her unless I'm totally sure I can handle it. Not to mention Valentine's own ability to handle my life, which is almost never a sexy cakewalk of a fling. I'm starting to realize that she can bounce back from anything, though. Flour. Mexican food. Even surprise sausage deliveries.

I don't know how long it's been, but eventually I have to turn off the light. My eyes are begging for some country darkness—this is pretty much the country—and the last thing I need is a ridiculous electric bill.

Easing out from under Valentine turns out to be the easy part. Once the light is off, and the only thing filtering into the room is a pale moonlight, I stand at the side of the bed, trying to figure out how to get back underneath her without waking her up.

I fail.

She stirs as I slide my arm back under her, a little smile curling at the corners of her lips. "Hi," she whispers.

"Hi. You can go back to sleep."

Valentine yawns. "Did you get a job or something?"

I laugh. What kind of question is that? "I did...but why does that matter right now?"

She shrugs against me. "It doesn't. It's just that your muscles are even...better than usual."

"Oh, thanks," I say, pretending to be offended. She laughs a silent laugh against me. "You *would* notice that I'm even more ripped than usual."

"How could I not?" She smiles, her teeth white in the darkness. "I think I'd like to notice everything about you."

"That doesn't make any sense."

"You do the talking, then."

I shift downward in the bed so that my head is actually on the pillow and breathe her in. "What do you want to talk about?" We're heading into territory that is decidedly not the kind of thing you get into when it's just a fling, but here in the dark with her, none of that matters. I just don't give a fuck about the rules of the game. Fling only...what does that even mean?

"Tell me about her."

My heart pounds in my chest—it's like I can feel it clamming up when Valentine asks the question. But I'm pretty savvy. I know how to avoid a grenade if I need to. "Who?"

She swallows. "Minnie," she says, and my entire body relaxes.

I don't bother to disguise the smile. "She's amazing." I think of her fine blonde curls at the back of her neck, the way she's endlessly adventurous, the way it doesn't seem to faze her at all that we moved cities. But it's hard to talk about Minnie without mentioning Angie, and I think—I *think*—that's what Valentine really wants to know. "She's...she's the only good thing to come out of a bad situation. Her mother's name is Angie."

Valentine frowns—I can feel it against my chest—but she doesn't say anything.

"I knew Angie from school a little bit, and when I came home from Afghanistan, she was still hanging around the town I grew up in," I say, every word measured. I have to figure out how to do this in a way that's not going to make it seem like I spend all of my time thinking about fucking Angie. "I didn't know it at the time, but she was a drug addict."

Valentine tenses against me. "Oh, no, Ryder," she whispers. It doesn't have a happy ending, that story, and she already sees it coming. But here we are. Now that I've started telling her, I can't stop.

"She wanted to move to the city, and I went with her. That was about three years ago." I shake my head. "Things went south. Things were really, really bad, Valentine." It's the first time I've admitted it out loud to anyone. "She went totally off the rails. The drugs—" I don't like to think of the way she was. Violent. Too violent. She'd come after me, and what could I do? The police would never have been on my side. So I'd let her have at me. Better me than somebody else. "Then she got pregnant."

Valentine sucks in a breath.

"When Minnie was born it changed everything. She was such a sweet baby. So bright. So interested in everything and everyone, but Angie didn't want to have anything to do with her. She tried, but she just wasn't cut out for... being a mom in that way, I guess. But it was different for me." I swallow down the ache in my throat. "A few months ago—five, maybe? — she went to work for a shift and didn't come back." The shame comes hot and thick. "I tried to make it work, but Minnie was beside herself. I couldn't leave her in daycare for long enough to make the money I needed to keep our place." There. I've said it. I've admitted my failure to Valentine.

But she doesn't move. She only holds on tighter.

"So now we're here. And I've got the job with my brother, for the time being, just until we can get back out again."

We both breathe quietly for a few long minutes. Is she asleep?

Then Valentine speaks into the dark. "I'm sorry that happened to you," she says softly, her voice a balm on the ache in my chest. "But I'm glad you're here. I wish you didn't have to leave."

Chapter Thirty-One

VALENTINE

WHEN I WAKE UP AGAIN, RYDER ISN'T THERE, BUT THE sheets are still warm from where he was laying.

I curl into them, basking in the scent of his skin, like Old Spice and sunshine, and then laugh out loud. Even thinking that a man smells like sunshine is unbelievably cheesy.

But he does.

After a few more minutes with my eyes closed, I open them again. My heart is beating faster even though nothing is going on. Where is Ryder, anyway? If he stepped out to use the bathroom, it's been a while, I think. I strain my ears, listening. There's a low rumble from the front of the house, toward the living room.

There's a gray haze coming in through the window. Who's he talking to? It's early as hell in the morning.

I wish he would just come back to bed.

I try to fall asleep again. Sooner or later, he'll be back here, and then we'll...

Well, we have a lot of options for things we can do. At least until his daughter wakes up. Today's my day off this week, so I don't have anywhere to be. Oh, shit—*he* might have somewhere to be. Jamie Harrison is his brother. I know Jamie from the couple of times he's stopped by the Short Stack, usually to buy one of the loaves of banana bread Gerald makes on Thursdays. And he does...oh, right. Jamie does lots of shit. He's kind of Lakewood's cute, nerdy jack-of-all-trades. I'd bet anything he has Ryder working for the lawn maintenance portion of his business. That would explain the muscles.

The minutes tick by, and with every one that passes, things seem a little less cozy-lazy-morning and more... *something's off.*

I stand up and throw my legs over the side of my bed. I have very little clue where my clothes from yesterday went. I think the panties were destroyed back at the Short Stack...oh, and the flour. The *flour* ruined everything. Somewhere, my outfit is in Ryder's washing machine. Or dryer, if he's really on top of things. I pull open his top dresser drawer and take the first t-shirt I see. There's a pair of boxers underneath. Good enough for me.

I head toward the bedroom door with a funny little smile on my face. This summer has been absolutely ridiculous, but at least it's a nice change of pace from Conrad's faux-seriousness paired with his ultimately assholeish demeanor. I don't think I'd change any of it. It seemed terrible to have to go back to waitressing, but at least Sharon didn't give me a hard time. It could be worse. I could still be suffering in the city under Conrad's influence. Gross.

I reach for the door at the same time that it flies open, hitting me in the forehead. I whip my head back, making it more of a glancing blow, but I still reel backward.

"Shit," says Ryder, coming in after me. "Oh, shit, Valentine, are you okay?"

I pull my hands away from the line of pain on my forehead and check for blood. His hands are already on my face, pulling me close so he can look. The worry in his eyes makes my chest feel warm. The last time I saw Conrad, he looked at me with such a cold gaze that it scared me. Conrad's never been worried for me. He's always worried for himself.

"I'm sorry," Ryder says and draws me in for a kiss. First on the forehead, then on the lips.

But something is off. I was right.

I pull back. "Wait. Are *you* okay?" It's only then that I notice that he's ashen, his skin a terrible pale color underneath the tan he must have gotten from working outside. "Ryder, what's wrong?"

"I'm so sorry I did that to you," he says, staring at my fore-head. I wonder if there's a mark. It's not bleeding, at least.

"It's really okay." The pain is already receding. "It was more surprising than anything else. But you don't—" I don't want to say he doesn't look good, because even pale and worried, he looks *good.* "You look like there's something wrong."

He looks past me, toward the window, and his jaw works. A strange desperation rises in my chest. I *really* want to know what's wrong with him. But can I press him? Is that part of this deal we've got going on? Or do I need to get my possibly wet clothes out of the washer and go back to my house while he deals with... whatever this is?

Ryder presses his lips together, and I think he might be get-ting ready to tell me to leave. I'm already leaning toward the door-way, thinking I'll head to wherever the laundry room is and get those clothes, when he speaks. "I got a call."

I pull back. His voice is flat, but still tense somehow, and it's making me nervous as hell. "From who?"

"A police officer in the city."

This is making no sense unless Ryder is secretly a criminal. But no. They don't go around calling criminals. That's...not a thing. "What did he say?" I take Ryder's hand in mine and squeeze it, gently, until he looks at me. "You don't have to tell me about this if you don't want to. I can just go if that's bet—"

"*No*," he says fiercely, his eyes flashing. "Don't go." He takes in a breath that looks like it's supposed to steady him, but he's still so pale. "They—they found Angie's body."

Angie. Angie, Minnie's mother. Angie, his ex-girlfriend, the one who walked out on him not that long ago. It didn't sound like a good situation from the beginning, but I can't imagine...I can't imagine.

"They need me to go identify her."

At that moment, Minnie wakes up, her small voice piercing the air. "Good morning, Daddy! Hey, Daddy? Where are you?"

Chapter Thirty-Two

RYDER

WE BOTH STAND IN THE BEDROOM, LISTENING TO MINNIE call out to me, and my heart shatters for her. It feels like it's dropped out of my chest and onto the floor beneath my feet. I'm not even sure why it's tearing me up like this right now. I never expected Angie to be a good mother. When she was pregnant, I hoped she'd be able to pull it off. Once Minnie was born, I gave up on that fantasy.

I guess I didn't give up on it completely.

It's not like I was expecting her to walk through the door and just pick up where we left off. I wouldn't fucking want that, anyway. Angie and I were a disaster from the start. But as long as she was in the world, Minnie had a shot at someday getting to know her. As long as there was a chance, I didn't feel like such an unbelievable fuck-up.

Now she's dead.

Valentine's eyes are locked on mine, but I'm having trouble seeing her.

"Oh, God, Ryder." She squeezes my hand again and I look down in surprise like it's the first time. I feel like I've left my own body but I'm still here. "Do you want me to get her?"

For a second I think she's offering to go identify the body and I don't know why she'd even try to offer that. She's never seen Angie. This isn't a thing that she can do for me.

When I don't answer, Valentine lets go of my hand and touches my face. The gentleness makes me want to burst into tears. I'm not mourning Angie. I never loved Angie the way I love Valentine.

The way I *love* Valentine.

It's just so fucking complicated that I can't begin to think about it right now.

Valentine looks into my eyes a few moments longer, her cool palm against my cheek. I give in to the urge to lay my hand over hers and press it close, just for another breath or two. It's not the kind of thing you do when you're just having a sexy fling with a woman. What you do in that scenario is send them away with the dawn, maybe after another quick fuck in the early morning light. But Valentine is still, steady.

Then she moves past me, her hand brushing my shoulder and down to my arm as she goes.

I stand there like an idiot and rub my hands over my face.

Valentine gets to Minnie's door a moment later. "Hello, sweet girl!" She sings out the words like she's done this a million times, and it makes my heart ache...but in a way that's almost pleasant. Definitely didn't expect *that*. "Good morning!"

"Hi!" Minnie cries out the greeting. There's a muffled squeaking—she must be jumping up and down in her Pack 'n Play—and then a giggle.

"Oh, my goodness," says Valentine. "It's morning! Did you know that?"

"Morning!" says Minnie.

"What would you like to wear today?" There's a pause, and I can imagine her eyes flickering around the room, looking for Minnie's clothes. They're in a dresser I found at the thrift shop last week, and sure enough, there's a sound of wood against wood. "Oh, this shirt is so *cute*! It has a dinosaur on it. And these blue shorts would be *great*!"

"My dinosaur shirt is *so cute*," echoes Minnie. Then their voices blend together, Valentine's leading the way.

I should go in there and tell her that I can handle this. I *can* handle this. I've been handling it mainly by myself—even when Angie was around—for Minnie's entire life. But something about this moment is almost too much. I let the sound of them chatting wash over me, and then I step into the shower. I'm going to have to go to the city, and I probably shouldn't look like some kind of hobo when I show up to...wherever it is I'm supposed to show up. Everything about that phone call has blurred together into a meaningless fog, so I'm going to have to call back and ask what I'm supposed to do.

God. That's going to be a hell of a phone call. Who has to call back the police to ask about their dead ex-girlfriend? Who has to do that? A spike of anger runs hot through my chest. What the fuck, Angie? You couldn't even stay clean for the *hope* of seeing your daughter grow up?

I've never felt so torn apart in my life, and it's not because I have any fond memories of her. I have a few, but they're like looking at pictures of someone else. They were so fleeting, and so rare, that it's like they never happened at all. The front she put up when we first met was a good one. It didn't last. By the time I realized it was all fucking fake, it was too late, and I didn't think—

I turn on the shower as hot as it will go and step in. I didn't think I had a real chance at someone else. At a better life. Not once I moved to the city with her.

I shower robotically, clean hair, clean body, and pull out the first available clean clothes from my dresser. Jeans. A black t-shirt. It's hot, but I don't want to wear shorts. I have no idea if my outfit is appropriate for identifying a body. I mean, what the fuck? Who has to think about this? I thought I left all that death and destruction behind in Afghanistan. Or at least behind in the city. No dice, though. It's still following me here.

It must have taken longer to shower than I thought, or maybe Valentine is an efficient angel, because when I come out to the kitchen, Minnie is in her high chair, eating pancakes. Valentine stands at the stove, making faces at Minnie while she flips pancakes.

A smile comes to my face in spite of...all the other bullshit. "I thought you were a waitress."

Valentine sticks her tongue out at me. She's wearing my clothes. I didn't notice before. Hers are still in the washer. "Gerald taught me a thing or two."

"The chef at that restaurant?" I move behind her and wrap my arms around her waist from behind, pulling her close.

"Yeah." She leans back against me. This is *not* casual fling material, but neither of us wants to say it out loud, apparently. Not in this kind of a moment. "He used to be in the Army, too. Did you know that?"

"No," I murmur into her ear. "I don't care about anybody there but you."

"You're terrible." She pushes back against me just as Minnie finishes another bite of pancake.

"Daddy? Hug?" When I turn around, she's reaching her chubby little arms toward me, and my heart breaks all over again.

"Sure, baby." I kiss her cheek and then reach for a washcloth in the door next to the sink. "We've got a long day ahead of us." My throat tightens. "We've got to get ready to—"

"Go to the park!" Valentine claps her hands. "We're going to go to the park."

I shoot her a look. "You don't have to do this."

She puts her hand on my shoulder. "I do. This is better for everyone. Plus, it's my day off." She waves the spatula she's holding at the door. "Get going," she says, finally. "Leave the car seat. And hurry back, okay?"

I hug her tightly, again, kiss Minnie's forehead, and head off to the worst job assignment of my lifetime.

Chapter Thirty-Three

VALENTINE

RYDER HARDLY SEEMS TO HESITATE ABOUT LEAVING MINNIE with me, though it's clear he has a *ton* of shit on his mind. I'm still reeling a little bit from the news myself, and I never knew Minnie's mother. I'm not sure I would have wanted to. I'm not sure I ever would have had the chance, anyway, from what he told me.

The main thing is, Minnie is only halfway done with her pancake. I was hoping he would let her finish. But if I were in his shoes—and God, I hope I'm never in his shoes—I wouldn't want to put off the task at hand. Or maybe I would, but what good would that do?

I grin at Minnie, who claps her hands. "I'm excited to go to the park!" I tell her, flipping another pancake.

"Go to the park!" Minnie cries. "Go down the slide?"

"We can *definitely* go down the slide."

We linger over pancakes for another thirty minutes, and I think about Ryder driving alone toward the city. I honestly can't imagine what it would be like to go to the morgue, wherever that is in the city, and have a body pulled out and—

I shake my head. This is *not* the time to focus on the gory details of today. This *is* the time to take Minnie to the park.

"My name's Minnie," she tells me for the tenth time as we walk hand in hand across the front yard. I pick up her car seat—a pretty robust number with a handle on top—and carry it with us. We have to get across to my house, to my driveway, to my car.

Plus, there's the issue of clothing.

Minnie's content to dig through my clean laundry basket while I run a brush through my hair and get dressed. I'm dying for a shower, just a little, but it can wait until Ryder gets back. At least this way I can leave the scent of him on my skin a little while longer. Minnie chatters, telling me her name and asking me what mine is. "Valentine," I tell her, again and again. "My name's Valentine."

"Balontine," she says, dumping out the laundry basket. Before I can ask her to put it away, she's already moving the clothes back to the basket, piece by piece.

We put on sunscreen—the morning is full *morning* now, and less of the haze before dawn—and pack a lunch bag filled with snacks. I guess my instincts from my babysitting days are still with me because I've always kept buying kid-friendly snacks. Minnie almost loses her mind when she sees the container of blueberries in my fridge.

"Bwuebewwies!" she cries, clapping her hands, and then she clasps them to her chest. "I *love* bwuebewwies. I'm so happy! I'm so happy!"

I like this kid.

But looking at her, my heart aches. She's never going to know her mother.

I can't think about it too long because even if Angie wasn't a good mother, even if she wasn't a good girlfriend, she was *Minnie's* mother. And it sucks that she'll never have a chance to ask her questions. Even if they're hard, painful questions.

It's a long, lazy morning. I don't feel any rush, any need to hurry her, because what are we hurrying for? Ryder didn't tell me what time Minnie naps, but I'll just play it by ear.

I install the car seat while she plays in the grass, picking the little white flowers that grow in my yard. I probably trampled quite a few of these in my mad dash away from Ryder the other night. It seems like a lifetime ago. Once Minnie is buckled in, we drive back across the street to pick up her nearly forgotten diaper bag. It's just a gray backpack, and it takes me a couple of minutes to realize it *is* a diaper bag, but when I open it, I find it stocked with diapers and wipes.

197

Back in the car, Minnie's ready to go. She holds one of her baby dolls in her arms and beams at me. Before we pull out of the driveway, I look in the rearview mirror. Not for the first time, it startles me how much she has of Ryder in her—especially those big, blue eyes.

He could have taken her to daycare. He could have done any number of things, but he left her with me. My entire chest gets warm.

He trusts me.

It's something more, then, for sure.

For *sure*, right?

I don't have any more time to dwell on it.

"Playground?" Minnie says.

"Playground!" I say, and she kicks her legs, her sparkly shoes glinting in the sunlight, casting beams of light like little stars all over the interior of my car. Nothing could ruin her day.

I'm glad for that, at least.

* * *

The playground is deserted this early in the morning, which is nice. The beach, however, is not. There's a crowd of early morning swimmers, and they mostly keep to themselves. It's a plus, actually, because Minnie loves to point them out.

"Peoples swimming," she says before she goes down the slide, every time. And on the swing.

It's not a bad way to spend the morning.

When she gets tired, around eleven, we go back to Ryder's house. She finishes off the last of the blueberries and eats most of the grilled cheese sandwich I make her. I tick it all off in my mind in case Ryder wants to know. Lots of parents do, when they get home. Some don't. What kind is he?

Minnie goes down easy for a nap in her Pack 'n Play after lunch, and I do the dishes in the quiet house and watch the dust motes floating through the sunlight streaming in the windows. The entire world seems calm, but somewhere, Ryder can't possibly be.

I think about texting him.

I don't.

I sit in the reclining chair in the living room and rock back and forth, listening to the squeak of the hinges beneath me. When I can't stand it anymore, I pull a book off the shelf at the side of the room and read it. It's a mystery novel. I never see the ends of these things coming.

I get almost a third of the way through the book before Minnie wakes up.

"Balontine?" she calls, and I put down the book with a smile on my face. She has just the sweetest little voice. "Playground?"

I'm tired from the sun, but what am I supposed to do, turn her down?

Not a chance.

Besides, what could go wrong?

Chapter Thirty-Four

RYDER

I T'S PROBABLY ONE OF THE LONGEST AND MOST FUCKED-UP DAYS of my entire life, and I did two tours in Afghanistan, for God's sake.

I have to go to the Office of the Chief Medical Examiner in Brooklyn, which was roughly where our last apartment was located before I gave up the lease. There was no damn way I was going to be able to afford the rent and childcare for Minnie without at least some help from Angie, and she was gone. Now she's *really* gone, and I have to sit in some random office that could be any office in the entire city. It looks nothing like I thought it would look. I'd imagined some kind of, I don't know, medical facility. Instead, it's just an office building from the seventies.

Another thing that surprises me is the wait. I have to wait two hours in a little queue of people because apparently today is a busy day for dead bodies. It sounded urgent on the phone, so the fact that I have to sit in a little office chair outside some guy named Edward's door for two hours out of my life is jarring, to say the least, and fucking ridiculous, to say the most.

It gives me lots of time to wonder if I've done the right thing by leaving Minnie with Valentine.

I'm pretty certain that I've done the wrong thing the more I think about it. Valentine didn't sign up for a too-hot-summer-spicy-fling to end up babysitting my daughter while I identify my ex-girlfriend's body. I can't even think that thought without a shiver running down my spine. It's a thought that has no business in anyone's head.

But the main thing is Valentine.

She didn't seem to have any hesitations about staying with Minnie. I just *left* the both of them and drove away to the city.

I try to berate myself for it while I'm sitting there outside the office, but I can't bring myself to do it. If Valentine's not trustworthy, I don't know who is. Plus, Minnie seems to be into her. A day out of daycare won't do her any harm.

I sit and stew, hands folded in my lap, and try to keep my heart rate under control. It's been at least a few months since I've seen Angie—maybe even six, it's hard to say now—and part of me is afraid of what might have happened to her. I don't want to have to tell Minnie some horrendous story one day about the state of her mother the last time anyone bothered to say her name. Lying doesn't seem like the best option either, for future Minnie.

God, I'm so fucking pissed at Angie. She has—*had*—a beautiful daughter. Minnie's like nothing the world has ever seen. Why wasn't that ever enough for her? Why was she such a violent, self-centered person?

I work myself up into an angry tizzy, sitting in the office building's hallway. It seems fucking weird that this is where they keep the bodies, with the people ahead of me *finally* getting called back one by one into the office.

In what has to be the world's biggest anticlimax, there's no body.

It's just me and Edward. He slides a photograph of Angie's face across the desk toward me. "Do you recognize this person as Angela Molter?"

I look down at the photo. It's definitely Angie, all right, stringy brown hair and all. She looks like she's fucking sleeping, which is what she did whenever she had a spare minute. There was almost never time to play with Minnie or take her to the playground or anything else, but she *did* have time to get high and sleep.

The sight of her unleashes a torrent of feelings that threaten to sweep me away. I'm angry. I'm devastated for Minnie. I'm at a

203

loss for words. I'm unbelievably sad that I'll have to explain this to my daughter one day. There's no way I'm ever going to be able to take away the pain once she knows.

Not one of the emotions is love.

All of that is stored up, waiting for Valentine, who offered to spend more time with Minnie today than Angie did in the last year she was alive. I'd bet that's true. It's fucked up, but it's true.

I swallow the lump in my throat. My hands clenched themselves into fists without me realizing it, and I have to work to release them.

"It's her," I say, and Edward nods, scribbling something on the form.

He starts to ask me questions about arrangements for Angie's body, but I can't take in much beyond a dull hum. My back aches from sitting in that uncomfortable-as-fuck chair all morning. The rest of me is dying to get back to Valentine and Minnie. So instead of answering I scribble down a number that I'm almost sure is Angie's uncle's and walk out.

They can deal with this. I'm finished. I've wiped my hands of all of it.

I'm ready to move on.

* * *

My shoulders don't relax until I'm back in Lakewood, which is a surprise because I hate this place.

Only I don't think I hate it as much as I first thought.

There's no car in Valentine's driveway, and in the kitchen, I find a note.

Went to the playground—she wanted another round! -V

It brings a smile to my face. Minnie loves the hell out of the playground at the beach, and that's all that matters. That she's happy. That *both* of them are happy.

I turn around and walk straight back out to the car. The day doesn't seem quite so damn oppressive anymore. At the beach, I want to sit with my arm around Valentine, watch Minnie splash in the water, and tell her that we should make this something real. Something *more*. I don't know how I'll find the words, but she'll understand. That, at least, is a given.

At least, I think it's a given, right up until I pull into the parking lot and get out of the car.

Minnie's in a swing, laughing her head off, and Valentine stands behind her, giving her a push every time she comes backward.

None of that is the problem.

The problem is the guy that's standing just to the side of Valentine, smiling at my daughter, laughing in the sun. He's way too close. He's way too familiar with her.

No fucking way.

Chapter Thirty-Five

VALENTINE

I'M IN A NIGHTMARE. I HAVE TO BE. THERE'S NO OTHER explanation for Conrad showing up at this playground, right now, in the middle of the afternoon. There's no reason except that the universe hates me and wants me to know it.

"Valentine!" He'd called my name just after I got Minnie into the swing and for one glorious second, I thought it was Ryder. But something about the tone seemed off, the voice was too high, and of course, it wasn't him. My entire soul shriveled when I saw who it was, but I didn't want to show that to Minnie. She giggled again and demanded another push on the swing.

"Ready, set, go!" I'd said, and she'd laughed as the swing went forward.

I couldn't bring myself to answer Conrad, but that didn't stop him from getting closer. "Valentine, hey."

"Hey," I said.

"How've you been doing?"

I stared at him.

"Ready, sec, go!" cried Minnie.

"Ready, set, go!" I said, pushing the swing. "Hi, Conrad." It was more of a struggle than I thought to keep my voice under control. "What are you doing here?"

"Seriously, Valentine?" He'd said the words lightly, with the hint of a laugh, but his voice made my skin crawl. Then he'd sidled even closer, which is the current situation. It's a conversation I *really* don't want to be having, but what can I do? Minnie is having such a good time. I can't yank her out of the swing without warning. I don't want Ryder to show up when I'm taking her away from the park in tears. I desperately want her to have a good day, so I push her again. "I told you I would be in town."

That must have been the text I got from him, but why would I pay attention to that when I was with Ryder? I almost laugh out loud, but then he'd want me to explain it, and I don't want to get into that. I *definitely* don't want to get into that. "I must have missed that part of your message." And *every* part of your message after you lost your damn mind over a *possible* pregnancy and then, oh, ruined my first-ever job.

"I think we should talk." Conrad crosses his arms over his

chest. He thinks the pose makes him look intimidating. At one time I might have found it vaguely attractive to see him like that, but now it makes me want to roll my eyes.

"I don't."

Conrad laughs. "You've always been funny."

I look at him like he's from another planet, which he might as well be. Conrad has *never* appreciated my sense of humor. Playful interludes were never his thing and forget banter.

"I'm not being funny." I have to keep my tone level because Minnie is hearing everything. She doesn't seem to have noticed the tension in the air. I silently thank God for swing sets. "We're over, Conrad. I don't think we should be talking." I nod at Minnie. "Plus, I'm busy."

"Babysitting?" He shakes his head, clicking his teeth. "God, Valentine. If I'd known you were running back here to pick up all your high school jobs, I'd have—"

"You'd have what?" My voice is too sharp, and Minnie swivels her head around to look at me. "Hi, sweetheart," I say. "A few more minutes on the swing, and then we're going to go get ice cream. Okay?"

"No!" she howls. Okay. Too late. She has to have picked up on the strain in the air, and, like every toddler, she's going to react negatively. Also, this is a great swing set. I can see why she doesn't want to leave, but we have to go.

I turn to Conrad. "There was no reason for you to do anything, Conrad. None whatsoever. What happened between us was private." It's coming back to me in a flood of shame, and I hate the blush that rises to my cheeks. It's a sick, embarrassed feeling. For a moment, I'm right back in the office, sweating through my skirt suit in front of my manager while he runs through some slick speech he's practiced for when he has to "let people go." I didn't "represent the integrity of the company." Never mind that it hadn't been what we thought. Never mind that I had been mistaken.

But Conrad—Conrad hadn't even been willing to give it a week. It was all said and done before my late period arrived. I'll never know if it was *really* a pregnancy—one of those early miscarriages—or just the stress of graduation and the new job. But what I'll never forget was the relief on Conrad's face when I told him. His words ring in my ears even now. *Thank God. Can you imagine what kind of mother you'd have been?*

There was nothing left to do after that but pack up and get out.

I take a deep breath. "I don't want to talk to you." I catch the swing, bringing it to a gentle stop. "Minnie, let's get some ice cream!"

Conrad laughs out loud, stepping even closer. I don't dare flinch away. I don't dare back up a single step. I don't know why the hell he's doing this, but when the laugh dies out his voice is urgent and strange. "I made a mistake, Valentine, can't you see that? I think you owe me a conversation."

He's standing so close that I can't lift Minnie out of the swing without running into him, and the last thing I want is for *her* to brush against him. I don't think about it, I just step in between them, putting my own body between his idiotic self and the swing. My back brushes against his chest and I flinch away. I don't want to be anywhere near him.

Conrad, though, wants to be near *me*. And it's at this moment that he mistakes my flinching, or deliberately misreads it, as some kind of excitement, reaches down, turns my face toward him, and kisses me.

I rear back, opening my mouth to snap at him, raising my hand to slap him, when he's yanked back away from me. The collar of his shirt pulls his neck back like he's a cartoon character and my hand swipes at empty air.

"Ice cream?" says Minnie and Ryder is next to her, out of nowhere, lifting her out of the swing. I'm absolutely flooded with relief. Now we can all get out of here, and—

"Sure thing," he tells her, pulling her close. But when I meet his eyes, there's nothing there but a bottomless rage. He's hiding it from Minnie, but barely. "Let's go."

Chapter Thirty-Six

RYDER

I'M SO ANGRY I COULD YANK THE SWING SET RIGHT OUT OF THE ground and swing it at this asshole's head. My muscles are tense, ready to follow through, but I can't. Not with Minnie here. Still, the rage is so white hot that it's threatening to burn me alive.

But it's Valentine that I'm so angry at that I can hardly speak. A thick disgust curls in the pit of my gut. What the fuck was she thinking, letting him get that close to Minnie? What the fuck was she thinking, kissing him?

Valentine moves quickly around to the side of the swing set, her eyes wide. There's a crackling urgency in the air now, and Minnie rests her head against my shoulder. She's always gone

AMELIA WILDE

quiet when things are tense, and I *hate* that things are tense right now.

But it's not my fault that Valentine decided to go ahead and kiss another man while she was babysitting my daughter. This was already the worst day I've had in a long time, and this is just the icing on the cake.

Then there's the thing that adds another awful layer to all of this. I don't have any right to be angry. I can be pissed as hell that she would do this in front of my daughter, but Valentine isn't mine. No matter how things seemed in the middle of last night, or early this morning, we still haven't had that conversation yet. We're not exclusive.

It doesn't matter.

My brain can't wrap itself around all this. All I can think about is getting back to the car. We have to go. I just threw a man down to the ground—a man who's picking himself up and brushing himself off as we move toward the parking lot.

"Hey!" he calls out, sounding half furious, half astonished. "Valentine!"

"Do you know that guy?" I can hardly release my own jaw.

"Yes." Valentine's face is stricken, but I don't care. I really don't care in this moment whether she's upset about getting caught. "But Ryder—"

"Valentine, we need to talk," he says, coming after us.

I whirl around to face him, and something in my expression makes him stop dead. "Don't come another step closer."

"Hey, Daddy?" Minnie's words are muffled by the side of my neck. "Ice cream?" My heart cracks into a thousand pieces. It's a sweet attempt to get us all out of this horrible tension, but it doesn't quite do the trick.

"Yes, sweetheart. Ice cream."

I turn toward the parking lot again, and asshole gets his courage back up. "Who the hell do you think you are? Valentine, stop. I wanted to talk to you."

"Where's the car seat?"

"In the back of my car," Valentine answers, fumbling for her car keys in her pocket. "It's right here. It's right here, Ryder." She clicks the door of her car unlocked with shaking hands and reaches inside to undo the seat.

He's not brave enough to come right up to the curb, but he lingers in the center of the lawn, watching us. Hurry up, Valentine. Hurry up, hurry up, hurry up. A deep cleansing breath does absolutely nothing, so I take another one. She gets the seat out of the car, and I step neatly out of her way. Mine is three spaces down. She goes toward it without hesitating, puts the seat inside, and fastens it, tugging three times to make sure it's seated.

Calm. Stay calm, just for a little while longer.

I never should have done this with her. I never should have gotten in over my head.

I give Minnie a squeeze, and she throws her arms around my neck and kisses my cheek. "Ready for ice cream?"

"Ice cream!" she says with a little smile. That's enough to get us out of here. I buckle her in, carefully, making sure the straps are exactly right. Then I shut the door and turn to face Valentine.

"I think we're done here."

Her mouth drops open, and the way she moves back half a step breaks something inside of me. But I can't take back the words, and I don't want to. I want to get far away from this place. Far away from this town. I want to get somewhere safe. I was beginning to think that boring, kitschy Lakewood might be that place. Not anymore. Valentine was a ticking time bomb, and the time just ran out.

"Ryder, I didn't want—"

I could yell at her, but Minnie is close by. "Would you have let that guy near your own daughter?" That's the rage my mind latches onto even though I'm not sure, even in this moment, that it's entirely justified. "God, what the hell were you *thinking*?"

She opens her mouth again, and then closes it, stepping back.

"Go have your conversation." I throw the words at her like weapons, and I see the look in her eyes when they land. "Just go, Valentine. We're done."

Valentine moves back another few steps, her eyes on me.

Well, she can look all she wants. I'm not going to come running back. I'm never going to come running back to anyone. She let me down just like Angie did. She chose something else over Minnie. And over me.

There's a part of me that's screaming to take her in my arms, to hold her close, to breathe in the scent of her hair and let it drown out the terrible wait in that office building, the pictures of my dead ex-girlfriend, all of it. But I take that part of me in my fists and shove it down so deep that I can't hear it anymore.

I just turn away from her and get into the car, pulling the door shut behind me. I resist the urge to slam it. Not in front of Minnie. No. Not in front of her.

I check behind the car, in all directions, three times before I put it in reverse. I pull carefully backward.

Valentine has moved over by the curb. She's still watching the car.

Come after me, that wretched voice calls. *Come after me, please, for God's sake, come after me and never leave.*

But Valentine's shoulders go down, and she turns away, walking back toward him.

Walking. Back. Toward. Him.

I'm done.

I'm *done*.

When I drive away, I don't look back.

Chapter Thirty-Seven

VALENTINE

WHAT. THE. HELL.

Ryder gets into his car and starts to drive away. He's being so careful with his driving—naturally—but he might as well have come after my heart with a butcher knife.

I feel like a fool for wanting to do all this for him. I spent all day feeling this incredibly deep connection with him. I cared for his daughter, making sure that nothing worried her at all. For her, this has been a fun, sunny day at the beach. And now, for me...

I should give him the grace to be an asshole in this moment. He just had to do something incredibly difficult. It's news that will be devastating to Minnie when she gets older, if not now.

But it's an ugly, hurt feeling in my chest that blooms and swells and takes over. His words ring in my ears, cutting me again and again. *Would you have let that guy near your own daughter?* I try to justify the words for him. I try to tell myself that he doesn't know it's Conrad. He doesn't know about the pregnancy scare. He doesn't know that I dodged a bullet by not having Conrad's baby. He doesn't know how devastating Conrad's reaction was, even though...

Fuck Ryder. He shouldn't have assumed anything. *I* shouldn't let my feelings get trampled by another man who wants to act like I'm a fucking failure at something I haven't even had the chance to try. How dare he?

How dare *they*? He and Conrad both clearly assume that I'd be a terrible mother and I have no idea why it smarts so much, but it does. It's like salt and acid on an open wound.

I'm sorry for myself for just long enough to turn around and slink back toward the beach. What am I going to do, anyway? Get in my car and then...drive out behind him? No. Not today.

As soon as I turn around, I hear him accelerate away, leaving me behind. My throat starts to close up. I have the wild urge to chase after the car, and it's ridiculous. I don't need to do that. We're not *there* yet. We never will be there. That's the thing I need to accept.

But I don't have time to accept anything. I don't even have

time to storm over to the lakefront and wade into the water so I can scream under the waves, where nobody can hear me. Because there stands Conrad, with some shit-eating grin on his face.

"Look, it's okay," he calls across the grass. "Come and talk to me. Not every babysitting job turns out. You can always get another one."

I stop, crossing my arms over my chest, and glare at him with every ounce of hatred in my body. "Fuck you, Conrad."

He pretends to act surprised. "My, my, Valentine, language." He glances around like there's somebody nearby to see, but the couple that was walking on the beach earlier is down at the other end now. Then he cocks his head toward the parking lot. His car is parked at the far end. I can't believe I didn't notice it before. "Come on. I'll buy you some food. What's that shitty Mexican place you love?" He laughs. "We can go there."

"You are honestly the worst person ever to live."

Conrad shakes his head indulgently. "Look, your feelings are hurt. That guy was a dick. Did you see him throw me on the ground?"

"*Yes*, Conrad. I was right there. Of course I saw it." I turn away from him. "Just leave me alone. Leave town. Find somewhere else to vacation."

I get exactly three steps before his hand is on my arm, yanking me back. "Valentine—" His voice is urgent. "Stop. Please. I made a mistake."

I tear my arm out of his grip and glare at him with gritted teeth. "Step. Back. I'm not going with you. Leave me alone."

This is what I should have done all along. I should have taken a stand for myself, back in the city. I shouldn't have let them fire me, not for that bullshit with Conrad. I should have made a huge fuss about all of it. I should have hired a lawyer.

I'm not going to bother with that now, but I don't have to stand here by the beach and listen to this any longer.

He opens his mouth to say something—one more thing, get the last word in, stay in control—but then shuts it. I whirl away and head for my car. If he follows me, so help me God...

I'm pulling the door open when he catches up to the curb. Not much in the world could deter Conrad right now, and my soul sags inside my body. I'm hurt and I have a headache. I've been in the sun too long. *Keep it up. Just keep rejecting him. That's all you can do.*

"Valentine, I'm not giving up on you. I gave up on you once before, but I'm not giving up now."

"Go home, Conrad."

"There's nowhere for me to go in the city," he says, louder.

"Your apartment should be fine."

"My dad fired me from the agency."

That makes my ears perk up. "Well, you probably sucked at your job." I reach for the door handle.

"I'm not going back," he says, sounding triumphant,

somehow, even in this moment. He's here for a consolation prize, and he *still* thinks he's come out on top. "I'm not giving up on you."

"Please give up on me," I shout, and then pull the door shut with all my might. It bounces off the metal clasp of the seatbelt with a clang, springing back open because of course it does. I tug the seatbelt in with a violent motion and shut the door.

Conrad stands right in front of the car as I'm putting it in reverse. "I'll never give up on you."

I feel my shoulders dip down. I can't fight him anymore, and certainly not from inside my car. I am on the verge of tears. I've never been more hurt, more angry. I am utterly defeated.

"Okay," I say, even though he can't hear me.

Then I drive away.

Chapter Thirty-Eight

RYDER

MINNIE IS HAVING THE TIME OF HER LIFE. SHE DELIGHTS over the ice cream shop and charms the owner, who gives her way too much chocolate chip cookie dough ice cream. I let her pick out every single piece of cookie dough. Whatever makes her happy. Someone should be happy on a day like today. Minnie should be happy every day of her life, but I know that's not realistic, so ice cream it is.

She's covered in melted ice cream by the time it's over, so I give her a bath. I can't say no to her. I can't bear to ruin even the slightest amount of fun for her, not today, not when her mother is dead. Not when I can't even mourn the loss of her because she was awful. But she might not have meant that to Minnie. I let her splash water all over the bathroom floor. I don't care. Water can be cleaned up.

I'm exhausted by the time we get to her bedtime story, which is six readings of the same book, over and over. She says most of the words with me, and every time she does it I burst with pride.

She's so worn out that she goes to bed without a fuss.

Perfect. Now I can dwell on what an asshole I was to Valentine.

I strip off the clothes I wore into the city today, wishing I had the energy to burn them and stretch out in bed. It still smells like her. God, she smells good. In the dark, I press my face into her pillow and breathe it in. How were things so good, and then so bad?

Leave it to Angie to ruin one more thing, even in death. It's a cruel thought. I don't like that I've thought it. But I'm so pissed at her and so dead tired, that I can't turn it around in my head. I can't be the better person that I—

Oh, shit. The better person that I am with Valentine.

I should go across the street right now and apologize. I make a half-hearted motion like I'm going to get back out of bed.

Fail. I just can't do it.

I try to reach for my phone, but my arms are heavy. Every muscle in my body aches. Heavy eyelids. Heavy heart.

I'll apologize to her first thing in the morning.

We'll go get pancakes.

She'll forgive me.

It'll be perfect.

* * *

Minnie is calling for me before I'm ready to wake up, but I've slept so deeply that I feel half-refreshed. Well, a quarter-refreshed. Let's not kid ourselves.

The sun is coming up on a hazy morning, the kind of summer weather that makes everything feel way too precious in a place like Lakewood. I don't have to be at work until noon. I called Jamie on the way to the city yesterday, and he said I didn't have to come in at all. Still, I should make up some of the hours, just on principle.

But first—

"Do you want to go get pancakes?" I ask Minnie, scooping her up from her Pack N Play.

"Yeah!" she cries, clapping her hands, and then it's all a game of finding her an outfit to wear, bundling her into the car, and driving away from the house. Valentine's car is gone, so she's definitely at the Short Stack.

My heart beats harder when we pull up into a spot right by the restaurant.

"Pancake breakfast," says Minnie solemnly, but then she breaks into a giggle. "Whipped cream!"

I think of that first breakfast at the Short Stack after a long and tiring night, and smile. It's not going to take long to get back to that. I'm sure of it.

I open the door and the bell jingles happily against the glass. Today is the day we're going to fix everything.

Sharon hustles out from the back, grabbing two menus on the way. "Good morning!" she sings, and then she sees me and the smile fades from her face. "Good morning," she says, and then smiles at Minnie. "I know just what you want. A Mickey Mouse pancake, is that right?"

"Mickey Mouse!" shouts Minnie rapturously.

Sharon nods. "I'll put that in. Sit wherever you'd like." She's still being friendly, welcoming, but there's something guarded about her expression that makes my stomach sink right down to my shoes. "Valentine will be right with you."

Minnie has only just started to color on her complimentary coloring page when Sharon comes out with her pancake. Minnie's eyes go wide. "Oooh!" Then she looks up at Sharon. "Cut it?"

I watch Sharon's heart melt—it's right there on her face—and she can't deny Minnie any more than I could yesterday. Without looking at me, she takes the seat next to Minnie and reaches for her silverware.

"Thanks, Sharon," I tell her, trying to add every ounce of sincerity to my voice. "Let me just—" I jerk my head toward the bathroom.

"Go ahead," she says, flicking her gaze toward mine. She doesn't believe me. I don't care.

I take the opposite turn, going out to the front room and through to the kitchen.

Valentine's standing just inside, tying her apron around her waist, facing away from the door. I creep up behind her and wrap my arm around her waist from behind, pulling her in, ready to feel her body relax against mine.

Instead, she tenses, spinning out of my grip and fixing me with a look that's pure disgust. "Ryder. What are you *doing*?"

I try to move toward her. "Making up with you." She moves back a step. "But it looks like you need some space."

She rolls her eyes, and it's not playful, not in the least. "I think we both need some space. I honestly don't know what you're doing back here, after yesterday."

"Valentine, I—" I have to swallow down an ache in my throat. There's hurt in her eyes, and I caused it. But the way she moves away from me is killing me. Even that first time we met, when everything was so painfully awkward and strained, she was always drawn to me. "I'm sorry about yesterday. It was—"

She waves a hand in the air, dismissing my words. "There's nothing we need to discuss about yesterday. You know, it was really—" She meets my eyes and stands tall, lifting her chin just a little. "It was a fling we were having. It's over now. No need to rehash it."

My instinct is to joke with her, to move closer, to make her laugh. I don't know how, but I have to make her laugh. Only I can't get close. She crosses her arms, standing back.

"Do you mean that?"

"Yes. I do." She answers firmly, and then moves toward the door, giving me wide berth. "Do you mind?"

I'm pretty sure I'm having a heart attack this hurts so badly. How did I not see this coming. How did I not *see*? Numbly, I step aside. "Lead the way."

Valentine moves out into the front room, head held high, back to me, and I come through the door after her. This is going to be an absolutely excruciating breakfast. I can't get out of it. Even from here, I can hear Minnie chattering to Sharon as she eats her pancake. There is no way on earth this could get any worse.

The door to the Short Stack swings open and both of us stop.

Valentine's mouth drops open.

It's that ass from the beach.

"Hey, Valentine," he says, lifting his sunglasses from his eyes. "I told you I wouldn't give up."

Chapter Thirty-Nine

VALENTINE

I TAKE A DEEP BREATH AND TRY NOT TO SCREAM, SWALLOWING A noise that would be fairly blood-curdling.

This is *not* happening to me.

Ryder snorts behind me, and Conrad presses his lips into a thin line. I can't see Ryder, but I'm sure that, like Conrad, he's puffing up his chest right now like there's going to be some kind of duel right here in the front of the Short Stack.

"You need me to—"

"Zip it." I hold up one hand, cutting off Ryder's words. He laughs, slipping around me to the side and going back to his table. Sharon passes him on the way, greeting Conrad before she looks at my face.

I look back at her, and then force on what I'm sure is an ugly smile.

She looks back at Conrad. Back at me. Back at him. She narrows her eyes.

Conrad puts on his most charming smile. "Is there a wait?"

I want to tell him that there is a wait, and the wait is forever, but Sharon smiles at him, tight-lipped, and grabs a menu. "We've got an open table in the back."

Well, thank god for small mercies, then, because at least he won't be in the front room with Minnie and Ryder. I don't want him anywhere near them. I don't want *any* of them at the Short Stack, but it's not like I could deny Minnie a pancake. Or anywhere else. I can hear her giggling over the noise of the other people who have filtered in. I have a bunch of tables, so maybe I can just ignore this entire thing, usher Conrad on his way, and try not to let it show that I'm royally pissed at Ryder.

"Valentine will be right with you," I hear Sharon say from the back room.

Conrad laughs. "Oh, I'm sure she will." Then he lowers his voice, mumbling something else to her. I don't catch any of it, only her eye roll when she comes back out to the front. Then she shoots me another glance. It's a glance that says *you're going to spill all of this the very minute the breakfast crowd is gone.*

I grab my notepad like a shield. Let's get this done with.

I approach Ryder's table with my head held high. I didn't let myself cry over his assholery last night. I just stayed up until four watching reruns of my favorite workplace comedy and drinking chamomile tea. He looks up at me, a rueful smile on his face, and damn it, those eyes...

I wasn't going to do this. I wasn't going to get sucked in again, get that pleasant-as-hell drop in my stomach when I saw him again. I was *going* to avoid him for at least a couple of days, but now he's here, looking at me, and God help me I want to sit down on his lap and kiss him right here in front of everyone.

"What can I get for you today? I see Minnie already has her pancake." My voice comes out leaden, and I clear my throat. "We've got omelets on special."

Ryder leans forward, scanning down the menu perched on the edge of the table. "How about an...I'm sorry omelet?"

"Oh, what a bummer. We're all out." It's far more sarcastic than I intended, but whatever, no going back now.

"What if I was really, *really* sorry?"

I don't have the time for this. "I'll give you a couple minutes to decide." I fix him with a big smile and turn away to the next table. It's hard not to look back at him every time I walk by. I definitely want to.

I get drinks for all those tables and put the orders in, and then it's time to deal with Conrad. I keep my attitude brisk and professional. He's not going to get the better of me. I'm done letting people get the better of me.

"Good morning," I say coolly. "What can I get for you to drink?"

"I want you back, Valentine."

"Drink. What can I get for you to drink?" I repeat the question louder.

"I told you I wouldn't give up on you, and I'm not going to give up. I'm right here."

The words are so damn hollow it's all I can do not to laugh out loud. Two months ago, I wanted those words from Conrad.

"Is there anything I can get for you to drink?" I give him a sympathetic look. "If you're not going to order, I'm afraid we're going to have to free up the table."

He levels his gaze at me. My stomach turns, and not in a pleasant way. "Coffee." Then he flips over the menu. So, this is his plan—camp out here with endless coffee.

"Coming right up."

I turn on my heel and make a beeline for the kitchen, grab the pot, and take a deep breath. My hands are shaking.

"Are you all right?" Sharon comes up and puts her hand on my shoulder. "Valentine, your face is red."

"I've got it," I practically shout. I'm not going to back down anymore. I'm not going to stand on the curb while a man drives away from me. I'm not going to be left behind, damn it, not anymore. I'll do the leaving. I'll get through this shift, and then I'll do the leaving, and they can all just deal with it.

I march back through to Conrad's table. He flips over the coffee mug that rests on his placemat. "Right to the top," he says as I pour the steaming liquid into the mug. "Yeah. You're a great waitress, Valentine. Amazing." He's supposedly here to win me back, and all he's doing is making snide remarks. Classic.

I just look down at him and finish pouring. "Did you want to place an order?"

"Yeah," he says, with a sneering grin. "For some of this."

Then Conrad reaches out and grabs my ass, squeezing it tight in his grip, like it's all his.

Chapter Forty

RYDER

I haven't been able to take my eyes off Valentine since I got here. Yes, it was indeed a mistake to try and fix this by hugging her in the kitchen. I want to do a lot *more* than hug her in the kitchen, but it's pretty clear that if I'm going to do anything, it's going to start with something a lot bigger than this.

I'm still trying to figure out exactly what that might be when she hustles through the room, not looking at me, coffee pot clenched in her hand. I can just see that asshole from the beach's table from where I'm sitting.

She pours the coffee, and I just manage to tear myself away. I don't need to be the person just staring at her like some kind of creep. Specifically, like *that* creep over there, who she clearly doesn't want to be anywhere near. It makes me sick to think that she's reacting to him just the way she reacted to me...

But she didn't. That's not how she reacted. Her face is set, eyes flashing, and I wonder if this is the ass who got her fired from her job.

Oh, my God. How could I have been so stupid? Of course it's the ass who got her fired from her job. I put both hands up to my hair.

"Uh oh," says Minnie, glancing at me while she scoops another spoonful of whipped cream into her mouth.

"Uh oh is right," I tell her, and I glance back toward Valentine to see if she's coming back through yet. I'll figure out something romantic right this second if she's about to walk back into the room.

Instead, I see the guy reach out for a fistful of her ass, right here in the restaurant, like we're not in public.

Hot rage bursts through my stomach, and I'm out of my seat before I even realize what I'm doing. If he'd do this in front of other people when she clearly doesn't want anything to do with him, what would he do behind closed doors? Get her fired, that's what. I don't know what his story is. I don't know what he could possibly be thinking, coming here, but I'm going to kill him.

I'm going to kill him, and it's going to be on behalf of the Valentine I met right here in this restaurant, the Valentine with puffy eyes and shoulders up to her ears, the Valentine who was so nervous about spraying me in the face that she almost didn't notice how much I wanted her.

How much I *still* want her.

I get three steps toward the doorway.

Then, in a movement as cold as I've ever seen, she extends her arm over his lap and tips the coffee pot, sending a stream of steaming coffee right onto his crotch.

"Oops," she says.

"Holy *shit*!" he shouts, jumping out of his seat and frantically trying to wipe the coffee off of his freshly ironed khaki shorts. I don't even have to know the guy to hate him, and I punch a fist into the air, barely stifling a cheer. "Valentine! What the hell are you thinking?"

"Do I have your attention?" she says, unflappable. "Do I have your attention, Conrad?"

Confirmed. It's him. I can't take my eyes off of the scene, and neither can anyone else in the Short Stack. Sharon hustles in silently from the front room and stops by my table, making absolutely no move to stop this. People all around me are forgetting that they should keep talking, and the restaurant goes silent.

"Quiet!" Minnie chimes in, and everyone laughs, but Valentine doesn't turn around.

"I don't want to be with you, Conrad. Not ever, and especially not now, when I am *at work*. At this job, which I never should have been ashamed to come back to. Sorry, Sharon." She says the last phrase over her shoulder.

"Apology accepted," says Sharon.

Valentine's focus is back on Conrad. "I don't know why you think I'd want you after your own father fired you. I don't know why you'd think I'd ever want a man who thought I'd be a terrible mother. If that pregnancy scare made you realize you were *dodging a bullet,* why would you even waste the gas to come here?"

Conrad is turning a deep red and still fanning at his crotch. He can't leave, because in order to do that he'd have to go past Valentine, who is still wielding the coffee pot, jabbing it toward him to punctuate her points.

Valentine's lip curls like she smells something disgusting. "I don't need you. I never needed you. It's none of your business if I came back here to get my life together, okay? I was mortified. And I was mortified because, for a split second, if you can believe it, I was *devastated* not to be having your baby. Now I know that I was the one who dodged the bullet. Just...get out of here, Conrad. The coffee's on me."

He opens his mouth and the entire cafe bursts into applause.

Valentine turns her back on him.

People start turning back to their plates, and the entire little cafe, this too-cute cafe in this too-cute town, fills up with chatter again.

But Valentine, who has never been too cute, who has always struck me as someone so deeply sexy that it made this place seem worthwhile, is still looking at me, her eyes locked on mine.

She's not done yet.

Chapter Forty-One

VALENTINE

I'M SO INCENSED THAT EVERYTHING IS COVERED IN A WILD HAZE of anger, like that coating of flour over our clothes the other night. So what if everyone in the Short Stack is watching the most awkward moment of my entire lifetime? Soon I'll be out of here, and everyone in Lakewood can talk about it with the tourists who are in here today.

I meet Ryder's gaze from across the room, and he's got such a silly grin on his face, so stupidly, fiercely happy, that for a split second I forget what I'm going to say. It's like I'm seeing his blue eyes for the first time. I still have that falling, flying feeling.

But I'm riding the wave of my anger, all that hurt, and I let it fly. For once in my life, I don't cower. Not even a little.

"And *you*."

He raises his hands in the air, his expression settling into something more serious. He doesn't try to interrupt, though I give him long enough to do it if he's going to.

"You were such a dick yesterday that I literally can't believe it."

The restaurant around us goes silent again. The side-eye quotient in here just went up by a thousand, and I'm standing right in the center of it. This time, though, Ryder is in the spotlight with me, and it's like people are just now realizing how insanely attractive he is. Out of the corner of my eye, I see one old lady at the center table by the wall lean over and whisper something to her friend, pointing her finger at Ryder.

Damn it, they're right. Even just standing there in his classic black t-shirt and jeans, he's making the temperature rise around us. I want to tear the shirt off of him and kiss him, push him back onto the floor, and have my way with him. I can't, though, because my heart is smarting, aching from what he said yesterday.

"I don't know why you're here either. I don't know why people think they can treat me like that, and then come crawling back like I'm just going to forgive what happened. No. Not this time. Not this time, Ryder Harrison."

He doesn't say anything. Silence, silence, *silence*. I'm expecting him to yell, to get red-faced and mean, but he doesn't.

Conrad slinks out from behind me, coming through the

doorway that I'm standing in now and cutting around by the side, both hands up like *I'm* the psycho in this scenario. He pauses in the other doorway, looks over his shoulder, and tries to get in one last word.

"You two are perfect together."

Sharon shoots him a glare that's enough to kill Medusa and points at the door. "Out."

There's some scattered applause. Part of me doesn't mind. This is Lakewood. What the hell else is going to happen today? Nothing this exciting, for sure. The other part is even more pissed that Ryder has somehow turned my job, this good, steady job, with a good, steady boss who would never fire me on the suspicion of being pregnant, into a sideshow.

"I'm done being blindsided by men like you." This one hits home, and I see it on his face, but I'm so bent on being heard that I don't care. For once, someone is going to care what I think. And if Ryder is collateral damage, so be it. "The fling is *over*. We are *over*." I'm saying the words loud and clear. Nobody will doubt me. Not after this.

Suddenly, it hits me, how very many people are staring at me right now. The Short Stack is not a large restaurant, but this is smack-dab in the middle of the morning shift, and almost every table filled up after Ryder got here. Every single person has their eyes on me.

It takes me right back to the agency on the day that I was *let go* for *not meeting the standards of the company.* Never mind that I had only been there two months. Never mind that I was meticulous in my work. Never mind any of it. I felt everyone looking at me on the way out of the office. They all knew what was happening. Everyone except me.

The next words I had to say stick in my throat.

"I—"

Ryder makes a movement, like he's going to come toward me. My heart throbs against my rib cage. If he touches me, I'm going to dissolve into a crying freak in the middle of the Short Stack.

I can't let that happen.

"Valentine—"

"No," I say, holding out my hand like a conquering hero. "No." Then, because this is so bizarre that honestly nothing can make it worse, I decide to just on out of this situation. I'm just going to leave it behind. Conrad, Ryder, the Short Stack—it's all too much in this moment.

The restaurant holds its collective breath.

Slowly, as if I'm in some weird hostage situation that I can only escape if I keep my movements precise and deliberate, I reach behind me and tug on the string of my apron. I catch it before it hits the floor and bunch it up in my hands. "This is embarrassing," I announce to all the patrons of the Short Stack. My voice sounds strange, like I'm announcing that there's been a severe weather update. "I'm going to go on break." Then, in case anyone missed it, I say it again. "I'm taking my fifteen minutes."

Not one person stops me on the way out. Not even Sharon.

Chapter Forty-Two

RYDER

T HE MOMENT VALENTINE IS OUTSIDE AND THE SCREEN DOOR swings shut behind her, Sharon springs into action.

The chatter breaks over the room like a wave. People around me are trying to figure out what the hell just happened. Two old ladies sitting nearby are beside themselves.

"Did you *see* that other one?" one says with a quiver in her voice. "What a disgusting dog."

"They both have their issues," her friend says primly. She drops her voice, but not quite enough. "And the attractive one is here with his daughter. I've heard that's his daughter."

I'm torn between running after Valentine and letting her go

forever. She can do what she wants. She can call it over if she wants to. I can't force her to be with me, and I would never want to do that. But the look in her eyes when she said those things...

It didn't look like it was over.

Still, the best thing I can do now is give her a little space.

I can hear Sharon's voice coming from the front room. "Emily? Hey, it's me. Can you come down to the Short Stack? Right now, yes. She had to...take a break. Fifteen minutes. No, I don't know. Just come, okay? I've got too many orders to—okay."

Then she rolls up her sleeve and takes over for Valentine. I pay for Minnie's pancake and, as soon as she's done eating, whisk her out of her high chair and out onto the sidewalk.

"I wonder where she went," I say out loud, slipping into my habit of narrating for Minnie.

"Where'd she go?" Minnie raises both hands in the air and looks in one direction, then the other.

"I don't know, sweetheart."

"Balontine come right back?"

"Maybe. But I don't know." I breathe in the fresh morning air, but all that does is make it easier to sigh. "I don't know."

* * *

Minnie and I circle the block, taking our time, but I don't see Valentine again. Either she's decided to just go home or she slipped

243

inside while we weren't on that part of the street, but it doesn't matter. I can't keep doing this all day. I'm going to look like the same kind of creepy stalker that Conrad was being.

No sign of him, either, which is about the only silver lining to this situation.

There's an ache in my throat that I can't get rid of, no matter how much Minnie makes me laugh, no matter how much she eases the tension just by being around.

I have to do something for Valentine. Even if she doesn't want to keep playing our game—even if *I'm* the only one who wants to take this to the next level—I have to prove to her that I don't think of her in the way she imagines. I have to. I might never see her again after this summer, and I can't have it end like this. I just can't.

Eventually, Minnie has to go home for a nap. The house is too quiet with her asleep, without any possibility of talking to Valentine, and I spend my little chunk of free time watching out the front window to see if she comes home. Her car isn't in the driveway.

At eleven-thirty, I have to leave for work. It just about kills me to leave without seeing her. I do it anyway.

I hate it.

* * *

"I don't know how you get yourself into these situations," Jamie says while he hauls another bag of premium garden soil out of the back of his truck. I'm still not in love with the idea of having to beg work from my brother, but of all the jobs in the world, this is probably the most ideal for the summer. It keeps me in shape and, most importantly, frees up my mind to think about Valentine.

I guess *dwelling* would be the better word, and somehow it's all mixed in with Angie. Valentine was there when I got that news. She was the one person on earth I trusted to leave with my daughter.

I look at him with narrowed eyes. He misses the expression entirely. "This isn't the same thing as with Angie." It's hard to say her name. It's always been hard to mention her to my family because it was so fucking embarrassing to be with her in the first place.

It's been five days since I had to go to the city. I haven't been back to the Short Stack, and I haven't seen Valentine's car outside her place. This morning I finally cracked and told Jamie everything.

"Isn't it?" Another bag of garden soil hits the pile with a heavy *thud.* "You pushed us all away so hard that you went all the way to Afghanistan."

"That's not why I joined the Army."

"Then why?" Jamie pauses and looks at me over the garden soil. "You always held everybody at arm's length. That's probably why you thought there was nothing for you at home."

"Mom and Dad wanted me out, and you know it."

"Nah," Jamie says. "You wanted to leave, and so you made that the story. It was easier that way."

There's a certain ring of truth to what Jamie's saying, something that feels way too familiar.

"I don't know about that."

He rolls his eyes, then reaches into the truck for another bag of garden soil. "Yes, you do. You're doing the same thing here. That's why you *have* to leave at the end of the summer."

"That's—" The argument is so flimsy that I can't force the words out. I hate it more than a little bit that my brother is right about this. At least, I'm pretty fucking sure he is. It's never been obvious to me until this moment, though, so my instinct is to scowl. "Fine. Maybe you're right. But that's not what's happening with Valentine."

"Look. Nobody can blame you for not wanting to rush things," he says, counting up the bags and reaching for the clipboard he has wedged in the back of the cab. "But if you keep pushing them all away, you're not going to end up with anybody."

Chapter Forty-Three

VALENTINE

"Cece, I have to get out of here." For just a minute, I give in to the urge and bury my face in my arms. I'm only halfway through my glass of wine and still feeling ridiculous.

"My friend," Cece says, coaxing me back into a sitting position. "This is not the end of the world."

I raise my eyebrows. "Not the end of the *world*, maybe, but work has been hell."

"I doubt that."

"Work has been *annoying*."

"I don't doubt that." Cece's eyes sparkle. "You really put on a show."

"That's not what I meant to do when I woke up that morning."

"Nobody ever expects to go into work and have a love triangle play out while they're on shift." Cece laughs at her joke.

I don't. "It's not a love triangle."

She forces her face into a serious expression. "I know. Tactless joke. I'm sorry."

"I forgive you. I guess." I reach for my wine and take another sip. I should be in a better mood than this. I finally stood up for myself and left both of them behind. I let out a groan that makes Cece laugh again. "This is horrible. I mean, it's good, but it's horrible."

I've been staying with her since my fifteen-minute break. After I got back to the Short Stack, Ryder was gone, but the heat in my cheeks lingered for hours. I couldn't bring myself to go home that night, so I went and crashed on her couch. Cece lives in a little blue house three blocks from the Short Stack, so it's convenient as hell to stay with her.

Plus, there's the added side benefit that running into Ryder isn't nearly as likely.

Of course, that hasn't stopped my body from *wanting* to run into Ryder. We were only having a fling for a few weeks, but it seems like longer than that. The desire that rushes through my veins whenever I think of him makes me think the amount of time doesn't matter so much as the way his eyes are like a sucker punch to my soul.

Don't think about him.

I last for a single breath.

"I know this is the right thing," I say out loud, looking Cece in the eye.

She purses her lips. "Do you?"

I slap my hand down on the surface of the table. "Are you seriously telling me that I should go back to one of those men?"

Cece wrinkles her nose, shaking her head so violently her hair shakes. "No. I am *absolutely* not telling you to get back with Conrad. He was a douchebag, and you know it. Everybody knows it. Everybody in the entire *town* knows it."

"Thanks for the reminder," I grumble the words into my wine glass. This is just not how I expected the summer to go.

"Valentine." Cece's voice is soft.

"Yeah?"

There's sympathy in her eyes. I will only ever tolerate sympathy from Cece. Nobody else. Well, maybe Sharon. But other than those two, no. I don't even want my mother to pity me.

"You know, you don't have to follow through on this."

"Follow through on what?"

A glass of wine with nothing to eat is going to give me a headache. I'm not hungry. I haven't been hungry for days, but it's just not the wise choice to skip out on food. Cece's ordered some fancy bread and dip—so typical of this wine bar—and I take a piece, dip it, and put it into my mouth. It's tougher than I thought, so I end up chewing it like a total cow while she looks at me, her gaze getting more sympathetic by the second.

"Stop looking at me like that," I tell her through the bread. "Follow through on what?"

She folds her hands on the tablecloth. "On your big... announcement."

I roll my eyes. "I'm not taking it back. Do you know how many people watched me tell Ryder we were over?"

"What does that matter?"

"It doesn't." I shake my head as an ache beats in my chest. "It doesn't. But what does matter is that he was a total dick, just like Conrad."

Now it's Cece's turn to look skeptical. "*Just* like Conrad?"

"Yes," I tell her. She's supposed to be on my side, and here she is, giving me the third degree. "He *also* accused me of being a terrible mother, which is stupid, because I'm not a mother yet." My voice breaks on that second *mother,* which surprises me so much my hand flies to my throat without my permission.

"Shit. Val—" Cece gets up and comes around to my side of the booth, sliding in next to me. "I'm sorry. I shouldn't be pushing you like this."

"No." I straighten up, dabbing at the corners of my eyes with a napkin and crumpling it into a ball. "Push me. I need a fire lit under my ass to get the hell out of here. I've been wasting so much time with—" I can't even bring myself to say it because it's so false. None of the time I've spent with Ryder has been a waste, even if it's not going to lead to anything.

That thought is the bleakest one of all.

"I've wasted a lot of time just focusing on the cafe, and not looking for other jobs." It's a lame cop-out, and Cece knows it, but she's my best friend. She doesn't say a word.

She just goes back to her side of the booth and picks up her glass. "To getting out of Lakewood," she says, and we clink our glasses in a silence that doesn't seem very festive. Cece bites her lip. "But Valentine…"

"If you're going to give me more advice, do it right now before I've had any more to drink."

"Just don't leave until you're sure that's the best thing."

"Why wouldn't it be the best?"

Cece shrugs. "I don't know. Maybe running away isn't all it's cracked up to be. Maybe you should give the place a chance."

It's hard to say, but I get the impression she's not just talking about Lakewood.

Chapter Forty-Four

RYDER

MINNIE WAKES UP IN THE MIDDLE OF THE NIGHT TWO nights later, howling about a lion, I think. When she finally settles, snoring in her Pack 'n Play, I can't go back to sleep.

I'm at a loss about what to do about Valentine. It's probably better, in the long run, that it ended up like this earlier rather than later. What were we going to do, move in with each other?

The fantasy hits me so hard I almost feel possessed by it. Valentine's voice in the kitchen with Minnie. Coming in from the yard after mowing the lawn. They're eating lunch in the kitchen together, peanut butter sandwiches and crackers with grapes on the side. Valentine's red hair shines in the afternoon light, in a loose bun at the nape of her neck, and I want so powerfully to twist my fingers through it and set it free from her hair tie that I can practically feel its weight in my hands. For once I don't have to think about whether or not it's the right thing to do—I just do it, and Minnie giggles when I kiss Valentine on the neck. I don't leave her out, either, planting a kiss on her round toddler cheek.

A movement in the yard across the street catches my eye, jolting me out of that impossible vision. It's ridiculous to spend the time thinking about it. It's never going to happen. It was never *supposed* to happen. We agreed to a summer fling. That was all.

The way it turned out anyway should be a lesson to both of us.

I catch another glimpse of the shadow moving toward the lakeshore, back turned to me, and just by the way she's walking, I know it's her. Plus, it's her yard so it would be pretty creepy if some other woman who looked just like her was walking around over there in the middle of the night.

I should just sit here. Or, better yet, go back to bed. I have work tomorrow with Jamie, and I'm going to need to get in extra hours if I'm going to accelerate getting out of Lakewood. That has to be the top priority.

I'm not going to go after her.

Nope.

I make it ten seconds before I'm out of the recliner.

First stop, Minnie's room. She's still snoring gently in the moonlight. Next stop, my room. I fire up the baby monitor app on my phone and double check that the app is working and she's still sleeping. She is. Phone, pocket. Self, door. After Valentine.

By the time I catch up to her, she's standing down at the narrow beach, a silvery glow caught in her hair from the moon. It takes my breath away.

"Bold move, Ryder Harrison."

She hasn't turned her head yet. I thought I was being fairly stealthy, but I guess not.

"What gave me away?"

"The sound of your front door shutting carries."

"Right." I move to stand next to her, my bare feet sinking into the sand. "Your parents have a nice property."

Valentine looks across at me, her eyes shining. "Did you come all this way to talk vacation homes?"

I give her a grin, but the look in her eyes makes my chest ache. "It wasn't very far."

She looks back out toward the lake. "No, I guess not."

There's a silence between us that's nothing like the silence as she fell asleep in my arms the other night. This one is tense, prickly, like we're both waiting for the other person to sink the knife in a little further. I don't know how it's come to this since this was never supposed to be anything more than fun, but it has, damn it, and I fucking hate it.

Valentine sighs. "We have to stop meeting like this."

Under any other circumstance, it would be funny, and I think maybe she meant it to be that way, but I can't muster a laugh. "I don't want to stop meeting like this."

She turns to face me and curls her arms around herself like it's cold out, even though it still has to be close to eighty degrees in the middle of the night. "I just don't think I can do it, Ryder. After—" Valentine shakes her head.

"After what I said? I was a prick. I didn't mean a word of it. It had been a long, terrible day." The words coming out of my mouth just seem useless. "But those are all excuses. I never should have said that to you, and I'm sorry." God, even when we're standing here like this in a deep freeze, I still want her. I want her even if it costs me everything.

"It's not that I don't believe you," she says.

A spike of irritation buries itself in the center of my chest. "If you believe me, why won't you just—" I laugh out loud, but it sounds harsh. "No. Fuck that. You don't have to forgive me for what I said."

"You're not the first person to say that to me." Valentine turns away again, back toward the water. She can't look at me. My heart plummets right down to the bottom of my shoes and keeps going until it burns up in the molten core of the earth. The pieces are coming together now—the asshole at the park, the things she told me about Conrad over our first fling-date at the Mexican restaurant.

"Valentine." I reach for her arm, and she gives my touch a

side-eye like I've never seen, but she doesn't flinch away. "You have to know...you *have* to know I didn't mean that. I would never have left Minnie with you if I didn't think you were awesome with kids. She took to you right away. I can't even imagine how amazing you would be with your own daughter."

"That's the thing," she says, quietly. "All of this—*all* of this—is happening because Conrad didn't think I'd be so hot. He told his father what had happened. He ran straight to him when I was..." She glances across at me. "Why am I telling you this now?" Valentine sounds bitter. "It doesn't matter."

"It does matter."

"Well, I've already started, so—" She blows a breath through her lips. "The reason we broke up was because a couple of weeks ago, I was late. And I told him. I was up front with him about it because we were a couple, and that's what you're supposed to do. You're supposed to be able to trust the other person, and—"

"And he decided to drop you like a hot potato."

She laughs. "That's a quaint way of putting it."

"That's what happened, though?"

Her face goes solemn. "I lost the job. I came back here. And I felt like such a fucking idiot for ever thinking, *oh, this might not be the worst thing if I got pregnant.*" She looks me straight in the eye. "Turns out, it would have been the worst thing, at least for him."

I open my mouth to tell her that it's not true, that he would have been the luckiest man in the world, but she cuts me off.

"I just need to start over. Completely. Somewhere new. And it can't be here, Ryder. It can't be with you."

I can't think of anything to say to that. I want to kiss her, but I'm sure she'd stop me, so I just step back and look over the water.

We're in silence for so long that I think she must be getting ready to make a move, to tell me that she's changed her mind.

When I turn around to look at her, she's gone.

Chapter Forty-Five

VALENTINE

WHEN THE SUN COMES UP, I FEEL SO WEIGHTED DOWN, SO awful, that it's a miracle I haven't slept. All I want to do is sleep, but I couldn't. I walked away from Ryder after many long minutes in the silence of the lakeshore, the waves lapping at the sand. He must have noticed me leaving because he shifted, putting his hands in his pockets, but he didn't turn around.

All the way back to the cottage my heart was pounding. With every step, I made another deal with myself. *If he comes after me now, I'll give in. If he comes after me now, I won't move out of Lakewood. If he comes after me now, I'll kiss him. If he comes after me now, I'll throw myself into his arms and go home with him.*

The disapproving Sharon-voice in my head thought this was

ridiculous. *If you want him, turn around and go get him. Just let it happen. You're being foolish.*

But I just couldn't commit to it. I'm not being foolish. I'm protecting myself. I should have protected myself way earlier from Conrad, and I didn't. Now I'm here.

I'm here, awake, looking out over the yard, looking at the sunrise over the lake, trying to make plans.

I text Cece.

Can I come stay at your place? I want to move out of here.

Some time goes by, I don't know how long, and she answers.

You know you can stay here anytime...

What are the dots for.

I don't think you should move out. Did you see Ryder?

Yes, and things are over. I can't stay here. If I keep running into him, I might never leave.

There are other options...

Again with the dots.

I sigh and lean my head back against the recliner. I made a cup of coffee an hour ago and forgot to drink it. I need to get to a place where this kind of thing isn't happening anymore. Maybe then I can get my career on track. Or start a new one. It doesn't matter.

With my eyes closed, my mind starts to wander, and it wanders right back to Ryder's bedroom. His body over mine in the dark. His hands moving over my body like he was always meant to touch me. His lips on mine, possessive and sweet all at once, never mind the rules about not getting in too deep. The pleasure. Fuck me, the pleasure. How it swept over me like waves, pulled me under like the deepest current, and brought me back to shore so I could fall asleep in his arms.

* * *

The harsh rapping on the outer screen door startles me awake, and I jerk upward with a snort. *Very* attractive. But the snort isn't nearly as attractive as the stream of drool running down my cheek and onto the recliner.

More rapping. I'd say it was a loud knock, but it literally sounds like the rapping an old crone would do in a fairy tale.

"I'm coming," I call. Ugh. My mouth tastes horrible. I pick up the coffee from the side table and take a swig, then let it fall right back out of my mouth and into the mug. It's ice cold and bitter. *Terrible.* "Hang on."

It's too bright for my taste, even though I'm not hung over or anything. I probably just *look* hung over. I'm still wearing the tank top and shorts I was wearing last night, and my hair has to be a mess. Well, whatever. This is my life now.

I pull open the inner door and blink out into the sunlight.

"This is pathetic," says Cece. She stands just outside, a paper bag from the local grocery store in her arms. "Let me in."

"What are you doing here?" It comes out as an even more pathetic grumble, but I step back and get out of her way.

"You're late for work, for one thing."

"Oh, *shit*." My hands fly to my hair, and I spin around in place, looking frantically for something to wear to the Short Stack. Skipping shifts is not my thing. Shit, shit, *shit*.

"Oh, my God, stop. Your work clothes aren't out here, for one thing, and Sharon agrees with me."

"Wait. Agrees with you about what?" I finally stop moving and face Cece. "What time is it?"

"It's ten thirty." She cocks her head to the side. "You started texting me at *four thirty* this morning. Clearly, you had been up all night because the Valentine I know would not wake up that early for a six a.m. shift. Not even a little bit."

I rub my eyes. "Yeah. You're right."

"I brought cinnamon rolls." She looks me up and down. "You're going to go take a shower while I bake these."

I give her a look. "You're not my mother. And I'm not an invalid."

"You've been moping for days, and you have weird circles under your eyes."

"I've been up all night."

"This is worse than when Conrad broke up with you."

"He didn't break up with me. We mutually—"

Cece holds up one hand. "Is this really worth going into? Go get in the shower."

"Fine."

I head into the bathroom and turn on the water. The moment I step in, I know that Cece was right. Going back to bed is only going to make this situation—whatever this situation *is*—worse somehow. Not that I know why I feel so heartbroken. We didn't break up. We might have been on the verge of being together, but that's not the same as a commitment.

What does it matter?

The thought comes to me while I'm rinsing the shampoo out of my hair. What does it matter if we were exclusive or not? Ryder left his daughter with me in his time of need. And before that, he made me feel like a fucking queen in bed.

That makes my heart sink. It's too late to be wondering this now, now that I've dismissed him in public and private and told him that it's over, over, *over*.

I get out of the shower and towel off, making at least a slight effort to put on some makeup. Then I put on my best jean shorts and a black tank top that will hopefully make it look like I'm not spiraling out of control over this not-breakup. Dressed, I head back out to the kitchen.

"Hey, Cece, I—"

No. Something's off. The house is too quiet.

"Cece?"

She's not here. Her car's not here.

There's just a plate of freshly baked cinnamon rolls and a note.

Don't let the past get the best of you. Take him some baked goods and make up.

You know I'm right.

-Cece

Chapter Forty-Six

RYDER

"MINNIE, SQUISH IT IN YOUR HANDS. LIKE THIS." I PICK UP a chunk of Play-Doh and squeeze it between my fingers.

Minnie watches me, then grabs a handful and smashes it hard between her palms. "Squeeze!" she shouts, then grits her teeth so hard her head shakes.

"I'm not a stalker," a voice calls out from the side of the yard, and both Minnie and I stop and look.

"Okay?" I call back, and just then a tall blonde with a grocery bag rolled at the top and shoved under her arm comes around the side of the house. She takes in the scene, looks at Minnie, and gives her a smile and a wave. "Uh, hi?"

"Hi. Your daughter *is* super cute." Then she seems to realize we haven't actually been introduced. Not even once. She must have heard about me from somewhere, though. I have a few guesses. She comes across the yard toward me and sticks out her hand. "I'm Cece Harwood." Then she gives me an expectant look.

"Should I...know you?"

She rolls her eyes. "God, she never tells anyone about me. It's like I don't even exist." She shifts the paper bag from under one arm to the other. "I've been Valentine's best friend since forever. I'm assuming you know who *Valentine* is, right?" Her eyes sparkle with the joke. I can see why she's Valentine's best friend.

"Yeah, I know her. And you know me already, don't you?"

"I know *of* you, Ryder Harrison." Cece looks me up and down. "And now that I'm seeing you up close—" She glances down at Minnie and decides not to say anything else. "Can I talk to you for a minute?"

"I think we're already talking." I like Cece instinctively, but I have no idea what she's doing here. All I know is that Jamie canceled some jobs for today, so I have an afternoon to spend with Minnie, squashing Play-Doh between our fingers and eating graham crackers straight from the box.

"Good point." Her eyes follow Minnie as she takes off across the yard, then runs back and grabs another fistful of Play-Doh, this time in a neon pink. "It's time to have a conversation with Valentine."

"We *had* a conversation last night. She was pretty clear about the fact that she wants to—"

"You two have to be the most frustrating people on the planet. Did you get a good look at her?"

"It was dark, I guess, but—"

"She's been sad for days, and honestly, I can't stand it." Cece shakes her head. "I don't know what you said to her last night, but she stayed up until dawn and started texting me about getting out town. Which is *ridiculous*." Cece looks me in the eye. "If she's going to leave town, she should do it with you."

My mouth literally drops open. "What—why? She told me last night that we were done. And it's not the first time she's said that. If she doesn't want to be with me—"

"What, you're just going to give up on her?" Cece clucks her tongue. "I know Conrad put on a big show, but that's not what she's looking for. I think half the reason the whole thing upset her so much is that she wants to hear that from you. All that shit with him—" Cece's face turns red just thinking about it. "She wants a man who's going to stand by her. And she wants a man who can do what—" Another glance at Minnie. "Let me just say that the gushing was almost as out of control as the moping."

I take a deep breath. "Listen, I appreciate the advice." My chest still throbs like I've recently recovered from a heart attack. The hope is just about killing me. "But I can't go talk to her right now. I'm...occupied."

"Oh, don't worry about that," Cece says, dismissing the concern with a wave. "She'll be stopping by soon."

* * *

I don't have anything planned, and I only half-believe that Cece could convince her, but I'm not a total fucking idiot. I see this as the last chance this is.

And I don't have anything.

All I can offer is a little bit of time. The very moment Cece drives away I hustle Minnie into the car and drive over to Norma's house. It's the middle of the afternoon, so the timing is weird, but she opens the door with a big smile. "Change your mind about work?"

"It's more important than work," I tell her, Minnie already running inside and joining the chorus of kids already playing. "I'll be back in a couple of hours."

Now I'm a little out of breath, sitting on my own front porch because I ran here from the car.

I don't know what to do to look casual. I sit down on the wicker furniture, and then stand back up, leaning against the door. That just feels weird, so I sit down again. No. I can't just be sitting there like an old man when she shows up—*if* she shows up.

Just when I'm starting to feel like an idiot for even beginning to hope that Valentine will come over, I see a flash of red move toward the middle of her yard.

My body instinctively assumes the most casual, cool position I can think of—leaning against the post of the porch, watching her move across the yard, her hips swaying with the beat of her walk. She's carrying a plate covered in plastic, and her hair is twisted at the back of her head. It looks wet. I wonder if she's been swimming.

Valentine catches sight of me watching her before she crosses the road, and I can see the blush spreading up her neck from here. She looks both ways and then crosses, holding the plate carefully level. Nobody can possibly blame me for the fact that in this moment I see her in a white dress, coming down the aisle with a bouquet of wildflowers.

She crosses the yard, not slowing, not speeding up, and comes to a stop a few feet in front of me. Despite everything, despite the stupid argument, despite the late-night dismissal, she bites her lip. I can see her breathing, the curve of her breasts just peeking out from beneath her tank top.

"Hey," she says. "I have cinnamon rolls."

Chapter Forty-Seven

VALENTINE

I'M OUT OF CLEVER THINGS TO SAY, AND THE OBVIOUS IS ALL I'M left with, so I say that. I'm too tired and too on the fence to be coy anyway. Thought I'd like to be coy. I'd like to be flirty and sexy as hell in this moment, no matter how this goes.

Ryder straightens up, a half-smile on his face. "I see that. I'm surprised you took the time."

"Oh, I didn't." She laughs. "Cece made them and left them out, with this note."

"A note?" His eyebrows go up.

"Is Minnie napping?"

He shakes his head. "No, she's at daycare for a couple of hours."

"Cool." I bob my head up and down, knowing even in the moment that I must look the most idiotic I've ever looked. It doesn't help that being this close to him is making me literally hot and bothered. I keep trying to tell myself—and him—that it's over, but standing here with these cinnamon rolls, it's clearly not. And it strikes me like a bolt of lightning over the lakeshore: I'm never going to be over Ryder Harrison.

What happened with Conrad, that cut me. It wounded me, but the wound was shallow. I healed it by coming back to Lakewood. I healed it by working at the Short Stack. I healed it by looking into Ryder's eyes.

When he said those same words, it struck me to the core of my soul.

It just about takes my breath away to realize why.

"Valentine?"

I've just been standing here, staring at the cinnamon rolls, as mute as the moment after I sprayed him in the face with that whipped cream. I tear myself away from the swirls of cinnamon and frosting and look up into those blue eyes, blue eyes like the endless sky, and swallow hard.

"Hi," I say.

"Are we starting all this over?" Ryder is full-on smiling now. He must see the difference in my face. Or maybe he's just looking at the circles under my eyes. "I can go inside and pretend I wasn't already out here."

"I really want to have your baby," I blurt out.

His eyes go wide, and then he bursts out laughing. I can't help myself. I laugh so hard that I start to double over, and Ryder leaps into action.

"No, don't!" he cries, reaching for the plate and lifting it out of my hands. "You'll crush the rolls."

He puts the plate in one hand and reaches for me with the other arm, slipping it around me as easily as if there was nothing between us but a too-sexy fling, pulling me in close. I rest my head on his shoulder and laugh until tears come to my eyes.

"No, stop," I say finally, stepping back. "That's not how this conversation goes."

He takes a breath and gets control over his own laughter. "How does it go, then? I kind of thought we were over."

"It hurt me so much, what you said," I try again, "because I...I've sort of fallen for you."

"Sort of?"

"I've really fallen for you," I say, watching the smile on his face deepen. "What I said before...I meant—"

Ryder pulls a hurt expression. "You *don't* want to have my baby?"

I laugh a little, but then I feel myself settle into a more serious mood. "I could see having a baby with you. I could see..." It takes me a few moments to find the words. "I'm not saying I need a baby right now. I'm just saying that I could see how it would be...it would be very joyful, with you. I think we could have fun." My throat tightens. "And honestly I'm not willing to give up on happiness yet. So—"

Ryder steps closer, pulls me in again, and kisses me on the side of my neck, just below my jawbone.

"I think what you're saying is that we should give this a real go," he murmurs, and the sound of his voice, the heat of the kiss, sends a shiver of pure pleasure down my spine.

"That's what I'm saying."

He kisses me properly then, his lips firm on mine. It only takes a few seconds for the kiss to deepen. Before I know it, my hips are pressed against his and his tongue is dueling with mine, and holy God do I need to get inside that house and get rid of these clothes. *All* of these clothes.

When we come up for air, I'm practically panting. "Let's go inside."

"There's one thing I have to ask you, though," Ryder says, leaning back just far enough to look into my eyes. "Are you okay with my... baggage?" Worry flashes in his eyes.

"Are you talking about *Minnie*?" I shriek. "She's the damn cutest person I've ever met, not a suitcase." He laughs out loud. "But yes. I'm okay with that. I'm more than okay with that. You guys are a package deal, and I want the whole package."

"I have a package for you..."

"God, Ryder," I smack his arm. "You're going to say this kind of thing to me out here? In public?"

He gives me an absolutely wicked grin. Then he lifts me up into his arms and backs up through the open door of his house. It's no sweat. He carries the cinnamon rolls in his other hand like it's no big deal. I can't stop laughing. I'm a puddle of liquid desire for him, but the joy is too much to be contained in silence.

Ryder takes us through the living room and into his bedroom, and there's a mad dash to get our clothes off, dumping them all in a pile on the floor. I leap back into his arms, legs wrapped around his waist, and he catches me like I'm weightless.

I bend my head toward his and take one more long moment to look into his eyes. The next couple of hours are going to be a whirlwind, I know, so that we can unleash all this tension built up between us, and I can't wait to have his hands on me. Our *life* together is going to be a whirlwind.

But right now we're in the calm before the storm.

"I love you, Valentine Carr," he whispers.

"I know," I whisper back.

He laughs and tips me backward onto the bed, falling with me onto the comforter like it's a big, soft stack of pancakes. I'm so desperate for him that I pull him in close, locking my legs around his hips and wriggling to get into just the right position.

"But really, I do love you," I tell him.

After that, we don't need any words for a long time.

Epilogue

RYDER

"ONE MINNIE MOUSE PANCAKE FOR MINNIE!" Valentine tries her best, but it's obvious that she's choked up. Lucky for her, Minnie is totally oblivious to everything but one thing.

"Balontine, more whipped cream!" She points her little index finger at the plate and then shoots Valentine an utterly charming grin.

"You know I've got it right here." Valentine adds several large dollops to the pancake and tries to pretend she's not fighting back tears. "And what about you? Can I put in an order for you?"

"Yes. One *final* order. Because we're never coming back here, not ever." I reach my arm out and pull Valentine close. She drops her arm over my shoulders, and we stand like that for a long minute. "An All-American Breakfast, please, mysterious waitress."

"Cece?"

Cece smiles from her spot across the table. "Pancakes. You know me. Just a big ol' stack of pancakes."

Valentine nods, bends down to give me a kiss and hustles into the back.

It's Valentine's last day at the Short Stack, and it's turning out to be surprisingly emotional. She's been teary since she woke up this morning—in my bed because she moved across the street to be with me after we realized it was more than a fleeting crush that we had on each other. *That* was about ninety seconds after we started *actually* dating.

It's been an absolutely crazy three months since then. We've both been working our asses off to save up money for our next adventure. We just found out last week what that was going to be. Valentine was hired to work in the marketing department of an up-and-coming publisher in the city—a hybrid magazine and book outfit that puts out all kinds of cool shit. I don't understand half of it, but it's the perfect job for her.

It does mean we'll have to move away from Lakewood, to Syracuse.

I've never seen Valentine more torn than when she got the

phone call offering her the job. First she jumped up and down, screeching with joy, and then her face crumpled. "But we'll have to move," she'd said, her voice muffled against my neck.

"Yeah," I'd told her, laughing. "It doesn't matter where we live. The important thing is being together."

"But I love it here."

"We can still love it here."

"We'll visit, right?"

"I'll have to get my cinnamon roll fix somehow, and Cece's are the best."

"Those were from the grocery store."

"Either way."

Now we're all here for her very last shift... and something else.

I'm trying to keep it cool for Minnie's sake. For everyone's sake, really. But it's proving to be more difficult than I thought.

"Breathe," Cece intones. "It's not going to be romantic if you pass out on the floor."

"I have been in *war zones*," I tell her, narrowing my eyes. "You think a little thing like this is going to take me down?"

"You can never tell," she says primly, and then dissolves into laughter.

Valentine bustles around the restaurant, filling glasses and putting in other orders. Cece keeps up a regular chatter with Minnie about her pancake, the stingy way they handle the chocolate milk at the Short Stack, and the various people walking by outside the front window.

Meanwhile, all my attention is focused on Valentine.

I'm glad she got the job in Syracuse. It's going to be fun as hell, and I'm finally going to get the chance to go to school and figure out what I want to do with my life aside from take her to bed with me every night. But she's an amazing waitress. This place suits her. Every time she stops at a table, everyone brightens up.

Finally, I sense in my gut that our order is about to be up. Cece must sense it too, because she gets up, pats my arm, and says, "Go get 'em," like I'm about to go finish out a golf tournament or something. She stations herself near the doorway into the back room just as Valentine comes out with our orders.

Valentine puts Cece's plate down first, then mine, and then tucks the tray under her arm. Her eyes are shining still, and suddenly I can't breathe.

But I do breathe because this is what I want my life to be. An endless series of days, looking at her gorgeous face.

"Is there anything else I can get for you?" She's trying her damnedest to stick to the script, and it's the most endearing fucking thing I've ever seen.

I glance down at my plate and then back up at her face. "Actually...yes."

Valentine frowns, scanning over the table. "Wait. Are you serious? Did I forget—what did I forget?"

I get out of my seat and take the tray from her.

"Ryder, I can carry the tray, it's just that—" Then she looks at my face—*really* looks at it.

I put the tray on my chair, and it clatters to the floor. Valentine doesn't even flinch.

"There's one thing you can get for me, yeah," I repeat, and then I get down on one knee.

Sharon has appeared in the doorway, and Cece is standing by with her phone, recording every moment and taking pictures as fast as her thumb can hit the button. All around us, breakfast patrons are catching on. The chatter dies down in an instant, and everyone is holding their breath, straining to hear what I'm going to say.

I should have planned this out in advance.

"Valentine." I start there. "This is where I first met you. You... sprayed me in the face with whipped cream, and I don't think you knew it then, but it broke me out of a long, dark, bleak mood that just sucked for everyone involved."

Valentine's hand goes to her throat, and a single tear slips down her cheek, but she's smiling so wide that it could power the whole city. *New York City*, not Lakewood. It's a huge smile.

"Everything before you—well, *almost* everything—was pretty terrible." This is the worst proposal speech I've ever heard, but it's straight from the heart and Valentine seems to know it. "But everything after—well, *almost* everything..." Everyone laughs. "... has been unbelievable and amazing. And I want that with you. I want that with you every day for the rest of our lives."

I take one last deep breath. "Also, I think it'll be much easier to sort out all the bills, and all those ridiculous emergency contact forms, and all the paperwork we'll inevitably have to fill out if—"

"Yes!" Valentine shrieks, jumping down into my arms and throwing her arms around my neck. "Yes, yes, yes," she says into my ear, and her tears are hot on my skin, and her smile is even bigger than before. "I will marry you."

"I was going to ask you if you wanted to have my baby," I say into her ear, and then she's laughing along with me, and everyone else.

Minnie sits in her high chair, beaming and clapping. She has no idea how good this is going to be.

"Ring," calls out Cece, and because this place is too damn cute, the rest of the patrons pick up the chant. "Ring! Ring! Ring!"

I help Valentine up off the floor, keeping my arm around her waist, and dig the small velvet box out of my pocket. When I open it, she gasps.

"It's not a diamond," I tell her, even though it's obvious by the garnet stones set into the band that it's *definitely* not that kind of engagement ring. "I hope you don't mind."

"We were never very traditional," says Valentine, and lets me slip it onto her finger for her which inevitably leads into a long, public, in-front-of-everyone kiss.

It's all a perfect fit.

To connect with Amelia Wilde, visit her online at

awilderomance.com.

Printed in Great Britain
by Amazon